COLUM McCANN

National Book
Award–winning author of
LET THE GREAT WORLD SPIN

THIRTEEN
WAYS
OF
LOOKING

A Novella and Three Stories

"Extraordinary . . . incandescent."
—*Chicago Tribune*

"McCann is a passionate writer whose impulse is always toward a generous understanding of his diverse characters."

—*The Wall Street Journal*

"Hauntingly beautiful."

—Associated Press

"The author of *Let the Great World Spin* has spent so long illuminating history through fiction that readers might miss the real source of his power: . . . his perfection of sentence, idea, and voice. [In these stories], all thematically related to a random assault McCann suffered last year, he displays a rare confluence of skill, style, and moral vision."

—*New York*

"Colum McCann doesn't write stories so much as compose sonatas, interweaving a range of rhythms and tonalities to create a luxuriant music. His new collection, *Thirteen Ways of Looking*, traces the journeys of his characters in lyrical prose that heightens the perils and losses they struggle to overcome. . . . Suffused with melancholy yet bright with beauty, the collection reaffirms McCann's stature as one of our essential literary voices."

—*O: The Oprah Magazine*

"The novella is an intriguing and suspenseful work. The three short stories that conclude the collection are extraordinary; in the shorter fiction his prose becomes incandescent, charged with the economy and lyricism of poetry. In one story, a mother and her adopted teenage son step into 'a shaft of light so clear and bright it seemed made of bone.' This is precise and evocative writing, strengthened by later events in the story that sharpen the analogy's menacing edge. Waves hurrying to shore are 'long scribbles of white,' and the unlatched bottom half of a door swings 'panicky' in the wind. As in Joyce's *Dubliners,* the psychological states of characters subtly color the descriptions of their environments, an artful mapping of inner worlds onto external ones."

—*Chicago Tribune*

"[*Thirteen Ways of Looking*] makes it clear that [McCann's] work is growing ever more textured and timely—and he has few contemporary parallels as a storyteller. . . . The stories in *Thirteen Ways of Looking* reflect an understanding of the swiftly disappearing flow of our lives as knowing and unflinching as any by Joyce or Chekhov."

—NPR.org

"Elegantly composed, emotionally charged and searingly perceptive . . . Throughout [the four stories], McCann makes us share his characters' pain and their eventual cathartic release, and he helps us to understand and appreciate that there is 'A lot of volume in this life. Echoes too.' "

—Minneapolis *Star Tribune*

"Stellar . . . a suspenseful and moving collection."

—*The Boston Globe*

"McCann is a gorgeous prose stylist, one who can establish an easy flow and then drop a sentence like this one: 'The roof over our love has been torn off and is open now to the endless sky.' Or this one: 'All the beginnings he attempted—scribbled down in notebooks—wrote themselves into the dark.' . . . His story

'Sh'khol,' included in *Thirteen Ways of Looking*, is as fine a piece of short fiction as I've read in the last five years. It's haunting and surprising, like everything from this amazing writer."

—*The Oregonian*

"[A] masterful Dublin-born author . . . McCann's wondrously meandering stream-of-consciousness style, which he employs for the title story (really a novella; it takes up more than half the book), owes a debt to James Joyce; echoes of 'The Dead' sound throughout, like a distant chorus of angel voices. . . . And in 'What Time Is It Now, Where You Are?,' a tiny masterpiece of writing about writing, we're in the head of a McCann-like author, sitting in his New York apartment, dreaming up a story. Ideas, phrases (one from Joyce, again) flit through his head; memories of his childhood invade the fiction he's creating. Ultimately the story becomes a barrage of questions about the characters he's birthed, pummeling like hailstones. He writes, in that quiet apartment, because he needs to find the answers. May those questions, from this most eloquent of wordsmiths, never end."

—*The Seattle Times*

"It is always a cause for celebration when Colum McCann, author of *Zoli*, *TransAtlantic* and *Let the Great World Spin*, brings out a new book. *Thirteen Ways of Looking*, his first collection of shorter fiction in over 10 years, [comprises] the title novella and three short stories. Each explores the role that chance plays in the lives of real people and all are written with empathy, humor and compassion. This is storytelling from a master."

—*Portland Press Herald*

"McCann's characters in this new work—whether nuns or judges or writers—are mostly ordinary people encountering extraordinary situations often touched by loss. Powerful, profound, and deeply empathetic, McCann's beautifully wrought writing in *Thirteen Ways of Looking* glides off the page."

—*BuzzFeed*

"In just three short stories and one novella, McCann weaves the magic that made *Let the Great World Spin* so acclaimed—especially in one brilliant short piece of metafiction in which the process of writing a story becomes interwoven with the story created."

—*The Huffington Post*

"A superbly crafted and deeply moving collection of fiction . . . underscores [McCann's] reputation as a contemporary master."

—*Kirkus Reviews* (starred review)

"Separate and together, these four works prove McCann a master with a poet's ear, a psychologist's understanding, and a humanitarian's conscience."

—*Publishers Weekly* (starred review)

By Colum McCann

Thirteen Ways of Looking

THIRTEEN WAYS
of LOOKING

A NOVELLA AND
THREE STORIES

—

COLUM McCANN

RANDOM HOUSE
NEW YORK

2016 Random House Trade Paperback Edition

Copyright © 2015 by Colum McCann
Reading group guide copyright © 2016 by
Penguin Random House LLC

Published in the United States by Random House, an imprint and
division of Penguin Random House LLC, New York.

RANDOM HOUSE and the HOUSE colophon are registered
trademarks of Penguin Random House LLC.
RANDOM HOUSE READER'S CIRCLE & Design is a
registered trademark of Penguin Random House LLC.

Originally published in hardcover in the United States by Random House,
an imprint and division of Penguin Random House LLC, in 2015.

LIBRARY OF CONGRESS CATALOGING-IN-PUBLICATION DATA
McCann, Colum.
[Short stories. Selections]
Thirteen ways of looking / Colum McCann.
pages ; cm
ISBN 978-0-8129-8658-7
ebook ISBN 978-0-8129-9673-9
I. Title
PR6063.C3355A6 2015
823'.914—dc23
2015011762

Printed in the United States of America on acid-free paper

randomhousebooks.com
randomhousereaderscircle.com

2 4 6 8 9 7 5 3 1

Frontispiece image © by iStock
Book design by Barbara M. Bachman

For Lisa, Jackie, Mike, and Karen.
For all those who continue to build Narrative 4.
In memory of my father, Sean McCann.

CONTENTS

—

Thirteen Ways of Looking   1

What Time Is It Now, Where You Are?   145

Sh'khol   159

Treaty   197

AUTHOR'S NOTE   243

READING GROUP GUIDE   245

THIRTEEN WAYS
OF LOOKING

I

Among twenty snowy mountains,
The only moving thing
Was the eye of the blackbird.

The first is hidden high in a mahogany bookcase. It shows the full expanse of room where he lies sleeping on a queensize bed among a heap of pillows.

The headboard is intricately carved. The bedframe, sleigh-shaped. The duvet, Amish-patterned. An urn sits on the left bedside table, a stack of books on the right. An antique lantern clock with exposed weights and pulleys is hung on the wall near a long silver mirror, freckled and browned with age. Beneath the mirror, tucked in a corner, almost hidden from view, is a small oxygen tank.

Half a dozen pillows are placed in the armchair, away from the bed. Several cushions rest on an oak chair with leather arm-rests.

The writing table sits near the doorway, with a number of papers neatly towered, a silver letter opener, a seal embosser, an open laptop. There is a pipe on the desk but no tobacco box, matches, or ashtray.

The artwork is contemporary: three urban landscapes, sharp lines and blocks, and a small abstract seascape on the wall by the bathroom door.

Amid it all, he lies lumpen in the bed, a blanket-shape, his head little more than a blur.

I was of three minds,
Like a tree
In which there are three blackbirds.

I *was born in the middle of my very first argument.* He should rise, find a notebook, scribble the phrase down, but it's frigid in the room and the heating hasn't yet kicked on, so he'd rather not move. But at least the sheets are tight and warm. Perhaps Sally came in to re-tuck him, since he seems, now, to remember the journey, or the several journeys, or—more to the point—the endless voyages to the bathroom. *I was born in the middle of my last epic voyage.* Above him, the ceiling fan turns. The handymen have reversed its usual spin. But how is it that a reverse-spinning fan creates warmth? Something to do with the updraft of air and the way a current flows. If only we could catch the draft, reverse our spin. *I was born in the middle of my first jury argument.* Strange to rethink the memoirs at this age, but what else is there to do? It was a surprise that the original book didn't sell well, back in the eighties, nicely published, nicely packaged, nicely edited. All the niceties. Even with a modesty pill he would have thought it would sell a few copies here and there, but it ended up, after three months, on the remainder tables. *I was born in the middle of my first public failure.* But when was it really, truly? *I was born the first time I made love to Eileen. I was born when I touched the hand of my baby son Elliot. I was born when I sat in the cockpit of a Curtiss SOC-3.* Oh, bullshit really. Bullshit with two capital *L*'s. Truthfully he was born in the middle of that first case when he stood in front of the Brooklyn court, a fresh-plucked assistant DA, and he shaped the words exactly the way he had dreamed, and they entered the air, and he could feel the way they fluttered, and what they did to the faces of all the all-male jury, and what they did, also, to the sympathetic judge who beamed with something akin to pride. *A very solid argument, Mr. Mendelssohn.* He knew right then he would never turn away. The law was what he was made for. How many eons ago now? He should write it down. But that's the problem with age, isn't it? You have the feeling, but not the dates. Find the dates, you lose the feeling.

A pencil and some paper, Sally, my dear, is that too much to ask? *I was born in the middle of my very first memory loss.* Why, oh, why is there is never any paper by the bedside? Maybe I should use a tape recorder? One of those little digital marvels. Perhaps there's one on my BlackBerry—it has, after all, everything else. He has taken, recently, to tucking it into his pajama pocket where it remains during the night, the little red light pulsing. A won-drous machine, it brings news of all the latest triumphs and ter-rors while he dozes and snores. Coups and wars and revolutions and rebellions and other sundry sadnesses all plotting their es-cape from the comfort of his bed.

Interesting that. They design the pajamas so the pocket sits on the left-hand side, over the heart. Something medical per-haps? A little compartment for the doctor to search. Somewhere to hold the stents and tubes and pills in case of attack. The ac-coutrements of age. He should ask his old friend Dr. Marion. Why is the pocket over the heart, Jim? Maybe it's just a tic of fashion. Who in the world invented pockets for pajamas any-way? And for what purpose? A place for a little extra bread or cracker or toast in case we get hungry during the night? A spot for the love letters from long ago? A slipcase for the alter ego, waiting, out there, in the wings?

Oh, the mind is wandering, plotting its escape: out the frosted window and away. And who was it, anyway, invented the cool side of the pillow?

He moves his toes a little in the sheets, rubs them together slowly, lets the warmth crawl up through him. He has never un-derstood the heating systems in New York. All these under-ground steam pipes and oil trucks and board meetings about boilers, and Nobel-winning engineers, and smarty-pants archi-tects, and global-heating specialists, a veritable brain trust, ge-niuses every one, and still all you get is a terrible clack clack clack in the morning. Dante in the basement, trying to prime the pipes. Good God, you'd think that in the twenty-first century they'd be able to solve the mystery of the fucking heating, excuse my French, my Polish, my Lithuanian, but no, they can't, they won't, never have, possibly never will. They don't turn the boiler on until five in the morning unless it's eastern Siberia outside. The building's superintendent is a chess master, hails from Sarajevo, once played against Spassky, boasts about his brain capacity, says he's a member of Mensa, but even he can't get the goddamn heating going?

He grabs the BlackBerry, keys it alive. Twenty-two minutes still before the pipes kick on properly. He is tempted to break his ritual, do an early check of the news and his e-mail, but he slides the BlackBerry back into his pajama pocket. *I was born in the middle of my first jury argument and I came out onto Court Street with a spring in my step.* Not quite true. There was never much of a spring in my step, even in those days. Always lagging a pace behind. Not quite Joe DiMaggio or Jesse Owens or Wilt Chamberlain or anyone else for that matter. The spring was kept coiled, instead, in the language, the intonation, the shape of his words. He sometimes stayed up all night at the mahogany desk, crafting lines. He had wanted, when younger, to be a writer. The fountain of Helicon. *I was born in the middle of my first contradiction.* Great arguments had nothing to do with substance. It was all about style. The right word at the right time. All fools know that a touch of fancy language can make any stupidity shine. In court he would study the jury's faces to see what fine words he might slip under their skin. The grace of an orator and the shape of a snake, said a colleague once, or was it the shape of an orator and the grace of a snake? A compliment anyway. Even a snake has its sibilant slither.

Eileen loved reading his judgments, especially in the later years, after he was promoted to the Kings County Supreme Court, when one newspaper or the other was always out to get him, *The Village Voice, The New York Times,* that chip-choppity New Amsterdam rag, what was it called? Not the *Brooklyn Eagle,* that's dead long ago. They cartooned him once as a praying mantis. He hated the face they gave him, the pouchy cheeks, the spectacles perched on his nose, the little round sling of belly as he chomped away on another praying mantis. Fools. They got it wrong. Only the female eats the male, after a bout of love. Still and all, it was hardly complimentary.

And why was it that they always portrayed judges as portly mountains of flesh? He was always as skinny as they came. A beanpole. A scarecrow. More fat, said Eileen, on a butcher's knife. But the cartoonists and even the courtroom artists insisted on giving him a bit of jowl, or a touch of paunch. It annoyed Eileen no end. She even started cutting back on the calories until he could hardly see himself sideways in the mirror. He used to think that the great grace of old age would be the giving up of vanity, but it is apparent even more these days: the sag of skin, the wrinkles, the eyes surprised by the sight of himself. He caught a glimpse in the mirror the other day, and how in tarnation did I acquire the face of my father's father? The years don't so much arrive, they gatecrash, they breeze through the door and leave their devastation, all the empty crockery, the broken veins, sunken eyepools, aching gums, but who is he to complain, he's had plenty of years to get used to it, he was hardly a handsome Harry in the first place, and anyway he got the girl, he bowled her over, he won her heart, snagged her, yes, *I was born in the middle of my first great love.*

He lets his arm fall over to the other side of the bed. *Saudade.* A good word that. Portuguese. Get you close, Eileen. Come snuggle in here beside me. Never a truer word. The longing for what has become absent.

She always said that his early court performances in Brooklyn were full of patience, guile, and cunning. A literary reference somehow—she was a fan of Joyce. Silence and exile. At home every morning she ironed his shirts and starched his collars and, with each case he won, she bought him a volume of poetry and a brand-new tie from the shop on Montague Street. He could have strung them from here to the Asian sweatshop: the ties, that is, not the poems. Eileen must have kept the Gucci factory girls alive, the number of cravats he had hanging in his closet, perfectly arranged, neatly coded and layered. Her dark hair, her pert little nose, the single mole on the rim of her cheek. She was lovely once and always, like the girl from the song. *Lovely once and always, moonlight in her hair.* There are times he still spritzes a tiny bit of perfume in her pillow, just to inhale and pretend she's still there. Sentimental, of course, but what's life without sentiment? And let's face it, when is the last time he had a bout of good old-fashioned lust?

Consult the BlackBerry, it will know. It does, after all, seem to know everything else: wayward sons, broken-hearted daughters, another spill in the Gulf.

He can hear Sally, already up and at it in the kitchen. The rattle of the spoons. The slide of the saucer. The touch of the teacup. The ping of the orange glass. The juicer being yanked from the cupboard. The soft sigh of the fridge's rubber tubing. The creak of the bottom drawer. The carrots coming out, the strawberries, the pineapple, the oranges, and then a serious clank of ice. The juice. Sally says he should call it a smoothie, but he doesn't like the word, simple as that, nothing smooth about it. He was on a shuffle in the park the other day—no other word, every day a shuffle now—and he saw a young woman at the park benches near the reservoir with the word *Juicy* scrawled in pink across her rear end, and he had to admit, even at his age, that it wasn't far from the truth. With all apologies to Eileen, of course, and Sally too, and Rachel, and Riva, and Denise, and MaryBeth, and Ava, no doubt, and Oprah, and Brigitte, and even Simone de Beauvoir, why not, and all the other women of the world, sorry all, but it was indeed rather juicy, the way it bounced, with the little boundary of dark skin above, and the territory of shake below, and there was a time, long ago, when he could've squeezed a thing or two out of that, oh don't talk to me of smoothies. He had a reputation, but it was nothing but harmless fun. He never strayed, though he had to admit he leaned a little. Sorry, Eileen, I leaned, I leaned, I leaned. It was his more conservative colleagues in the court who gave him the evil eye.

A bunch of shriveled-up prunes, or prudes, or both—how in the world, beyond party politics, did they ever get elected? What did they think, that a man must hide his life in the judge's shroud? That he has to pop the errant head back under the shell? That the only noise he'd make was the gavel? No, no, no, it was all about taking the rind of life. Extract the liquid. Forget the pulp. Juice it up. The Jew's Juice. A smoothie.

Oh, the whirl of the mind. Sorry, Eileen. I was passionate once, and that's the word. Flirtatious maybe even. Nothing more. Never one to harass. That was something he passed on to young Elliot instead. More's the pity. Look at that poor boy now. But enough of all that. It's no way to start the day, with his errant son, his wandering eyes, hands, ears, throat, wallet.

He can hear the faint ticking begin. Come, heat, hurry. Rise up the pipes.

Why is it that New York never produced some boy genius to solve the heating problem? You'd think that with all the children born in this thumping metropolis that at least one of them would get miffed about the clank of pipes and the hiss of steam? That they'd solve their everyday dilemma? But no, no, no. Off they go and make their millions on Wall Street and Broadway and in Palo Alto and Los Alamos and wherever else, and still they come home to an apartment designed for cavemen.

What is this godforsaken apartment worth anyway? Half a million twenty-seven years ago. Sold the brownstone on Willow Street and made the trek to the Upper East Side. All to make

Eileen happy. She loved strolling by the Great Lawn, taking her ease around the reservoir, going on jaunts down to Greenberg's bakery. She even put a mezuzah by the front door. To protect the investment as much as anything else. Two million dollars now, they say, two point two maybe, two point four, but they can't get the heating on before five in the morning? We can put a black man in the White House but we still can't get toasty? We can send a mission to Mars but we have to freeze a good man's co-jones off on East Eighty-sixth Street? We can fit our BlackBer-rys into our heart-side pajama pockets, but we can't guide the steam up through the walls without a racket?

Oh, but here it comes, here it comes. The first click of the day. As if there's a man down there wrenching open the pipes. A second tick. A third. And then a whack. Crash bang wallop. Good man, Dante. A divine comedy indeed. Abandon all hope. Jazz in the heating pipes. If only. Wake me up, Thelonious Monk. Come dwell a while in my steampipes. Visit the basement while you're at it.

—Sally!

He can hear the juicer crunching through the ice, the stam-mer of the blades, and the clack against the glass container.

—Sally!

The juicer gradually slows down, the sounds softening into silence.

—Sally, I'm up!

Which, quite plainly, he is not. Neither one way or the other.

They have installed a hanging white bar at the side of the bed and a few other gadgets to help him levitate in the morning. Elliot even wanted to put a hoist in at one stage. Like he was some sort of giant shipping container. *You need a hoist, Dad.* A hoist, my ass, dear son. A hoist needs hoisters and not just for the oysters. Eileen, quite clearly, would not be impressed: she liked poetry of an altogether different order and she never quite cottoned to his cheap little rhymes. She was a fan of that Irishman, Heaney, and she had a penchant for another wild head of hair named Muldoon. She would go to their readings every chance she got. Chasing down the boisterous bards, it always made him smile. He himself saw both poets at a Waldorf dinner once: they should have written a rhyme about the rubbery chicken and the slippety-slop waiters. He crossed the room, stood in line, took out his good fountain pen, got the poets to sign a cloth napkin, and tucked it away—he was afraid that he'd get caught white-handed, a judge to be judged—and he brought it home to Eileen who clutched it to her nightgown and then kissed him a worthy goodnight: I'll see you in my dreams.

But that's. Some. Fucking. Noise. This. Morning. But here, at last, the hard hiss of steam. He can feel it already begin to flood the room. Good morning, Thelonious. Time to rise. And shine. Make God your glory glory. Katya used to sing that to him long ago. Along with her dreidel rhymes.

He grabs hold of the bar and swings his knees across, scoots himself up in the sheets and goddammit it all to hell. He can feel it now, under his pajama bottoms. She has put him in a pad. Yes, a pad. Plain and simple, by any other word, a diaper. Why the hell does she do it? A goddamn diaper. And when in the world did she slip it on? How did he possibly forget? He can remember the sound of the traffic on Court Street fifty million years ago, he can remember Heaney at the Waldorf, Muldoon too, he can remember being born as a young lawyer, for crying out loud, the tie shop on Montague, Katya and her nursery rhymes, he can remember boarding the SOC-3, but he can't remember Sally slapping him in a diaper just this morning?

The dark dogs of the mind.

—Sally!

Long and tall she is indeed, but quick on her feet she is not. Not the girl to sally forth: sally eighth more like it, sally ninth.

—Coming, Mr. J.

Well, so too is Hanukkah. So, too, is the twenty-second century. So, too, is the end of the visible world. Hurry on and help me, woman. A goddamn diaper. Why the hell did you sling this forsaken piece of foolishness on me? What did I do to deserve it? What crime? What cruelty? A diaper! I might have needed one eighty-two years ago, that's true, Sally, my dear, and forgive my Polish, my Lithuanian, my half-baked Yiddish but for fucksake, woman, I hardly need one now.

He is halfway out of the bed and virtually suspended in midair when he hears a little wheeze and the rumor of a sigh, and then footsteps in the hallway. A slow shuffle. Sally stops, perhaps to catch her breath, and it takes him a moment to figure out whether she is moving towards him or away. The clockwatch. The waterboil. The plodalong.

The cruelty of time. Never enough of it when you need it. And always too much when you don't.

—Sallllly!

Another sigh, an audible *Uh-huhn,* four more steps, and then the turn of the gold-plated door handle.

—Here I be, Mr. J.

Here she is, here she be, and have they no grammatical rules in Tobago at all? They mangle the language. Mingle it. Mongrel it. No *Chicago Manual.* No Strunk or White. Sally will never make it onto the pages of *The New Yorker,* that's for sure. Nor the *Times,* nor even the *Daily News.* She might scrape up a position for herself at the *Post,* but only just, by the hair on her chinny-chin-chin.

Yet there is something lovely about her cadence. She speaks with bright coins in her voice. A tambourine in her throat. She swallowed a bird, Sally James, the first of the morning. In she breezes, cool as a treetop, tall as a redwood, sturdy as an oak. Her shape above him in the bed. Her dangling earrings. Her hair sticking out at fantastic angles. Half her life spent on that hairstyle. Curlers and irons and combs and all sorts of accoutrements. In the early days he could hear her getting up at four in the morning, just to get ready, curling, blowdrying, stitching, braiding.

She has a peculiar smell to her, a good smell, like furniture polish, dear Sally from Tobago, or is it Trinidad? And how, anyway, do they differ? And who, quite honestly, gives a flying fig? Does it matter if she's north, south, up or down, east or west, when the simple fact of the matter is that he is wearing a diaper and it must be removed, hastily, quietly, *now*.

How in the world did it happen, Sally? What hour did you sneak up on me?

Imagine that, my pajamas down around my ankles, the pocket still over my heart, the BlackBerry clock, tick-tock, and I wonder what she thought, or thinks, of my equipment? I am not a man of great fire-hose potential. She has seen it now, uncoiled, or coiled, how many times. Seahorsed. Hooded. We can only hope that the living don't snicker.

—Sally?

—Yes, Mr. J.?

—Did I really need the winter gear?

It has become his little phrase: the winter gear. The idea of calling it a diaper galls him, and an incontinence pad is too much of a mouthful, or rather a handful, or a bucketful. And what is it the British call it? Such a fine gift for language, the British, having learned how to use it from the Irish, or so Eileen always said. But even the great linguistic masters fail here. A *nappy*, by all accounts. What specimen of genius came up with that for crying out loud? What learned Oxford mind? After a napkin no doubt. Fold it up. Tuck it in.

—Sally, I don't like it.

—It's so you don't spoil your sleep, Mr. J.

—Well, it sure as hell spoils my waking.

She rears her head back and shows her mouth full of dark fillings, but this is no laughing matter, Sally, no laughing matter at all. Here's me. And there I be. She is bending down towards me, her sharp perfume, her tickling hair, and she draws back the duvet, performs a quick whipaway of the sheets. Oh, is there anything worse on God's dark earth? He shifts sideways on the bed and he can tell right away. Lock me up, Your Honor. Throw away the key. Oh, Lord, you pissed and shat yourself Mendelssohn. Who owns this body, this foul little wreckhouse, this meshuggeneh mansion? Who allows us this filthy comedy? Divine it is not. How in the world did I sleep through all that? The ancient pisher in me. A fountain of Helicon indeed.

She steadies him and reaches across for his Zimmerframe—who the hell was Zimmer anyway? He leans across and says that he'll do it the rest himself, remove the winter gear, ski to the bottom of the slope.

And then he says: Please.

Oh, smash this body entirely, Sally, break it up into little bits and pieces, and then I can walk around with the still-working head and heart, leave the useless pieces behind me. Fare thee well bowels, colon, pajama pocket, errant prostate, all ye untenable pieces. Let the Mendelssohn mind meander. Let the heart stroll. Leave the alter kocker behind. I have always gone according to the laws of nature. It's a naked child against a hungry wolf. *I was born in the middle of my very first diaper change.* Not even my first, truth be told.

He leans close to Sally again and he can feel her strong hefty arms and her hand at the soft of his back and who would have thought that the last lady in his life would have breasts as generous and as round as Sally's? Soft and fragrant. Round and juicy. Full and floppy. Oh, you're a good woman, Sally James, from Tobago, or Trinidad, or Jamaica Plains, or wherever the hell it is, and what is it I pay you again? I should make sure, double sure, triple sure, that there's something in the will for her, she's a good soul, she means well, though she has no grammar, but neither do I at times, *I is, I am, I was, I will be,* but, oh, she has me halfway in the air, it's all a matter of science now, lift me, bring me to the mountaintop, resurrect me, roll away the stone, and he can feel his body creaking forward, Sallying forth, and he half collapses onto the Zimmerframe and he heaves a big sigh of relief, even though he can feel the contents of the winter gear shifting down below.

—Steady, Mr. J.

—Just get me to the church on time.

—Huhhn?

—The bathroom, Sally. The bathroom.

—Yes, sir.

Dilate your nostrils, Mendelssohn. Hurry on now. Mach shnell. Enough creakiness. Give life long enough and it will solve all your problems, even the problem of being alive.

—You look pale, Mr. J.

—Never felt better.

—We forgot, she says.

She crosses the room and bends down to the walk-in closet. Stretching the white of her uniform into two neat halves. Oh, I'm a terrible man, but, Lord, there are indeed worse sights. Hear no evil, speak no evil, but at my age I should at least get a little peek?

—I forgot what, Sally?

Out she pops, all flesh and smiles, swinging a pair of slippers in the air.

—Oh, Sally, I don't need any stupid slippers!

—Mr. J.?

—Did you hear me? No slippers, woman.

She bends and taps his leg and gets him to raise his foot anyway.

—It's so you don't slip, Mr. J.

—This is not a goddamn ice rink, Sally.

She darts the whites of her eyes at him and he lifts his right foot in a gentle apology. Oh, Sally, but did you really have to choose the fuzzy ones? Isn't there a more subtle pair you could root out? Has my whole life come down to fuzzy slippers? Nor are they a perfect fit from Brooks Brothers. And did you really have to put a diaper on me in the middle of the night? And is my treacherous son in trouble yet again? Did something happen to my lovely grandkids? Is my daughter yet returned from her mission of peace?

He is glad, so very glad, that Eileen never had to see any of this. She checked out two years ago now, dearest Eileen. Imagine that, never smoked a cigarette in her life and ended up with the cancer all over her lungs. A quick, sharp exit. At least there was that. Exit ghost. Take Hamlet with you.

—All set, Mr. J.

Under starter's orders. The Zimmer race. Might as well get the checkered flag. Assume a virtue, said the Bard, if you have it not. When in the world did she start calling me Mr. J. when my real name is Peter, Petras, Peadar? She glimpsed my initials once, I suppose. Which is not all she glimpsed, more's the pity. Oh, Mendelssohn, you miserable fool. Solid as Peter's rock you are not.

—Thank you, Sally.

—Hhhrrrmmmpppf, she replies.

Be a mensch, Lord, and put me out of my misery. What an exertion simply to get to the bathroom. He maneuvers the walking frame over the trim piece, manages to close the door. He stands, holding on: there are handles all over the bathroom. An emporium of handles—handles for the sink, handles for the shower, handles to haul himself up out of the bath, handles for the handles.

He nudges off the slippers, opens the drawstrings of his pajamas and lets them drop to his feet, steps slowly out of the puddled cloth. The string tangles around his big toe and he almost stumbles but he catches himself at the edge of the sink. A quick glance in the mirror. Hail, fellow, well met. That is not me. Nor even I. Good God, I look like a pair of old curtains with a great big valance under my neck. A rubbery thing, could stretch to eternity.

Onwards. Onwards now. Life is short, but it's the morning that takes all your time.

Clean yourself, Mendelssohn, get yourself together. Dignity and grace. *I was born in the middle of my first jury argument, though sometimes I feel I've been born at other times too.* And who in the world would be interested in a second memoir anyway when truth be told the first was an all-out flop? Ridiculous, really.

He reaches down and pulls at the side of the diaper. Careful now. Contents in the underhead bin may have shifted during flight.

Oh God, oh Lord, there's nothing worse than the sound of velcro.

There's nothing worse on this fair earth.

III

The blackbird whirled in the autumn winds.
It was a small part of the pantomime.

There are two cameras in the living room, both motion-activated. The first is hidden in the bookcase, the other well concealed on a shelf by the window. Both have fish-eye lenses, which gives the pictures a faintly maritime effect, everything stretched out on a moving wave.

When the curtains are opened, light flushes the room with a theatrical surprise. The focus is the large oak dining table, surrounded by six Chippendale chairs, hand-carved, fretworked. On the table sits a Chinese vase with flowers and a patterned dish that holds keys, letters, pens.

There is a large painting on the wall above the table, a portrait of Mendelssohn, wearing suit and tie, large-rimmed glasses, a serious gaze.

There are several other paintings in the room, eclectic in

style and taste, the most prominent one a Maine seascape. A Persian rug takes up an expanse of the living-room floor. An all-glass coffee table sits by a long sofa. The books on the coffee table appear to be floating in mid-air: Roth, Márquez, Morrison.

The rest of the room has an ancient lived-in feel: a dark Steinway with an open lid, a set of fire irons by the blocked-up chimney, an antique wooden bar with several crystal glasses perched on top.

Later the homicide detectives will be surprised by the presence of the cameras: they will find out that it was Mendelssohn's son, Elliot, who secretly installed the nannycams to keep an eye on Sally James, though there doesn't seem much reason to suspect her at all, nor much reason to watch Mendelssohn at the table, sipping his coffee and reading his paper, looking down upon himself from his own portrait, the older self looking considerably more wan.

They scrub through the digital video and watch the footage from the day of his death. Every now and then Sally James walks in front of the mantelpiece camera. She vacuums. She arranges cushions. She sits for an hour and reads a magazine. Mendelssohn himself shoves his walking frame into view exactly three times: once, when he shuffles to the writing table, reads a book, scribbles a note, checks his BlackBerry; another, when he shuffles to the window to check, presumably, on the snowy weather outside; another, when he stands in the room, in the early morning, staring vacantly ahead.

When he turns to the camera he is caught in the faded glory

of his maroon dressing gown. He has the lined cheeks, the hooded eyes, the frugal smile of age, but there is still something of the robust boy about him, the way the memory of his body still appears to move under the skin.

The detectives watch Sally emerge several times into the living room, slow and laborious. Each time it takes a moment for the aperture to adjust. A backlit blaze, then a slow darkening. She wears nurse whites and slippers. She is broad, sturdy, with an undulation to her shoulders. A large hip-sway. No malevolence to her, no impatience. Nothing untoward or suspicious. She comes in, puts down the early morning smoothie, sets the table for toast and coffee, hands him the newspaper, returns again with a jar of marmalade. The footage is chilling only because it is so ordinary.

Nor is there much in the way of interest, or evidence, later, when she helps Mendelssohn into his overcoat, wraps his scarf, dons his hat, takes his elbow, and walks him out of the living room.

They will watch Sally when she returns to the apartment to see if she betrays any further emotion, but she simply sits in the armchair, puts her feet on a footrest, reads her magazine. Later, when she receives the news in a phone call, she will throw her arms to the sky and rush through the living room, turning once to retrieve her coat and shoes. In the late afternoon, she will pace the floor, and when the news of his death is confirmed, she will fall grief-stricken to her knees.

There are so many ways to go, the detectives know, opposition and conflict, theories drifting over and beyond one another. Things changed by the act of observation. The old laws of physics. Speed and position. Time and distance.

They will comb through the images, looking for any random detail, the breeze of surprise, a clue. The more obscure the moment, the more valuable the knowledge. There is always a chance they will spot something they already overlooked.

They work in much the same way as poets: the search for a random word, at the right instance, making the poem itself so much more precise.

IV

A man and a woman
Are one.
A man and a woman and a blackbird
Are one.

Used to be there was quite an art to the newspaper fold. Back in the days when they summered out on the Island. A young whippersnapper. Sitting on the LIRR with the other suits and ties. It was a spectacular skill, to be able to fold the paper in long neat sections. The choreographed commute. An early morning ballet. They could sit in rows of three, knee to knee, turn the pages and still never touch elbows. Streamlining it. Some of the more meticulous could make perfect folds right along the story-lines, four little corridors of broadsheet, like the fine edge of a bespoke suit. When the world was respectful and polite. Brief-cases and umbrellas and door-holding. Occasionally there was a schmuck who couldn't fold the paper at all and he would be there, arms flailing, paper rustling, no respect, an accordion of elbows, the same species who could never find his commuter pass, or who dropped his coffee, always fumbling around, making noise, causing a fuss. At least in those days there were no cell phones to deal with.

He took a train up to Stamford last week to Elliot's house, his mansion rather, awful place, twelve bedrooms and swimming pool and media hall and five-car garage, but cheap and shoddy all the same, like the one next door, and next door to that, a row of Ikea houses, such wealthy mediocrity, his very own son, his big bald son, who could believe it? The baldness, the bigness, the stupidity, in a house designed to bore the living daylights out of visitors, no character at all, all blond wood and fluorescent lighting and clean white machinery, not to mention his brand-new wife, number three, a clean white machine herself, up from the cookie cutter and into Elliot's life, she might as well have jumped out of the microwave, her skin orange, her teeth pearly white. A trophy wife, but why the word *trophy*? Something to shoot on safari?

Just as well Eileen never got to meet her. She wanted so much for her big, tall boy and what did she get except no grandchildren, a boatload of sorrow, and two divorces? Not to mention the fact that Jacintha came with three boys under her wing, ready-wrapped fatherhood, straight from the mail-order catalog, all legs and pimples and angst. His step-grandchildren, a blubbering stew of adolescence, he can hardly even remember their names, nor their faces, and who in the world would name their son Aldous these days anyway? A brave new world it is not.

Where was I anyway? The mind these days, it slides so quickly. *Nosce te ipsum.* Something to do with cell phones? Or was it the newspaper and the folds?

Used to be that he'd read the paper cover to cover, minus the sports, then fold out the crossword puzzle, finish it in twenty minutes flat. Not anymore. Still, it's one of his favorite moments of the day, the mental brunch of *The New York Times*. Open to a story about the Central African Republic. An awful thing, those machetes. All the news that's fit to splint. A report on North Korea. No money for the Super Collider. The imminent collapse of the Middle East peace process. Well, of course, there's always that. Hard to think of it collapsing since he knows full well that it was hardly ever built up in the first place. Poor Katya, over there, week in and week out, in her diplomatic post, pleading and cajoling and mollifying her heart out, when the plain fact of the matter is the bastards just don't want peace, any of them, one side or the other, Jew or Arab or Christian or Coptic or whatever else, they'd rather suicide-bomb one another asunder, it's the ordinary man on the street who suffers, women, too, not to mention poor Katya herself, over there with his teenage grandkids, no *step* about them, beautiful kids, Laura, James, Steven, but a life under the microscope, armed guards all over the estate, and why did she have to choose Israel of all places, couldn't she have gotten involved in Belfast or somewhere halfway sane?

Poor Eileen hated to see any news of Northern Ireland. Used to put her in an awful tailspin. Over there blowing the heads off one another for no sane reason either, lobbing molotov cocktails, marching in parades to celebrate the dead, flying their banners, King William up on horseback. All war, any war, the vast human stupidity, Israel, Ireland, Iran, Iraq, all the *I*'s come to think of it, although at least in Iceland they got it right. Odd that. You never hear a peek of war from Iceland at all, but then again who'd want to be firing bullets over a piece of frozen tundra?

Nothing but misery everywhere, truth be told. Why don't we say that the whole world's a madhouse and simply, then, leave it be? Isn't that right, Sally? I'd bet there's even some form of carry-on going down in wherever it is you're from.

—Sally!

She is busy down in the bedroom, vacuuming and singing her sweet head off. An eternity ago, my mother used to sing to me too while cleaning the house. Far away, far away. In the kitchen. The stove was large and red and potbellied. A giant stovepipe, painted blue for some reason. Standing there with flour on her hands. Wiping them on the front of her apron. All the old Lithuanian tunes. Mountain flowers and frozen canals and riverbanks and ferryboats.

Vilnius, Vilno, Wilna, Wilno. The world has a complicated geography. In later years his mother filled him in on the particulars of his birthplace—the knifeblade used for making ice skates, the way the moonlight fell upon the rivers, the small red jacket he always wore, the gloves she stitched with elastic inside his sleeves, how they bounced when he ran along through Kalnų Park. Once a dog chased him, attracted by the bounce of his gloves. Dark dogs everywhere. He had nightmares after that. Then the daytime itself installed the dark. They got out of the city just in time. His mother had a feeling of what was in the air. How many wars had there been already? Poor Vilnius, Vilno, Wilna, Wilno, renamed at every turn. How many times had it been run and overrun? A great dignified city, all yellow brick, high cornicework, but pierced with bullet after bullet. His father, a well-known doctor, sold the house on Vokiečių Street, took the savings, bundled the family on a train bound for Paris. It was still a time when borders could be crossed with ease. They had plenty of money to get by. No hidden jewelry. No blessings from the rabbi. No furtive prayers. No curses either. No ghetto-quarter narrative. No babies thrown from the windows. His mother had dropped nearly all tradition behind her. It didn't interest her to be Lithuanian, or Polish, or Russian or anything else for that matter, not even Jewish. His father, too, was a stern atheist. Not at all interested in the formalities, though he would sometimes read the Torah and even recite parts of the Kaddish, saying that lines of it were a recipe for great thinking. *In this holy place, and every other, may there come abundant peace.* Or something like that. Bow to the left, bow to the right. And it would be something indeed, wouldn't it? *Abundant peace?* Two chances, as they say: slim and none.

The steam train rattled past the tall thin trees of Germany,

Belgium, France. They lived in a hotel on the banks of the Seine. At night they gathered in the hotel kitchen, around the radio, the intimate fireside of the world, all that flaming hatred, ash, the sundering of Europe. The nights of long knives, the weeks, the months, the years.

But then it was Dublin, in the middle of the war. His father got a job in the Royal College of Surgeons. A city taking its ease under a bountiful sky. Applauding its own grayness. A hat of it, a homburg, a derby of drab. He loved it there. His happiest two summers. A house on Leeson Street not far from the canal. Ten years old, he wore shorts with garters and long elastic socks. Bobbed along the cobbled streets, came home to a warm fire in the early dark. A staircase. A long dining table. Two silver candlesticks in the middle. Oh, the mind itself is a deep, deep well. Lower me down and let me touch water. He even tried to acquire for himself a Dublin accent. Two chances there also: none and sweet fuck-all.

Out in the morning, he would run full tilt towards the canal. There were two gorgeous swans that twined their necks around one another. In the afternoons his mother took him for walks along the grassy banks where he was allowed to strip down to his undershorts and jump in, pale and skinny, with the other boys. For some reason he could never work out, he was called Quinn and then, after a while, Quinner. Maybe he looked like a boy of that same name, or perhaps there was a Dublin slang in it he didn't recognize, but he loved it, especially given the fact that a *Q* did not exist in his language. *Quinner! Hey, Quinner!* He wrote his nickname out elaborately in lined copybooks. Even his teachers latched on to the name, and when he handed in assignments he wrote Peter J. Quinn Mendelssohn.

Oh, it takes a lot of volume to fill a life. So said Boris Pasternak. Or at least I think it's Pasternak. Eileen would know. She used to read it aloud to me at night. The roof over our love has been torn off and is open now to the endless sky.

In Dublin one of his school reports had said that he had a youthful bent towards philosophical inquiry. A youthful bent! Philosophical inquiry! Eleven years old! Surely only the Jesuits were capable of a phrase like that. They saw great promise in him. Overlooked his background, slipped him books of Catholic substance. He walked home along the canals with Aquinas rattling around in his head. But on summer afternoons all he wanted to do was to jump off the dark canal locks, holding his knees to cannonball into the water. There was even a photograph taken of him on June 15, 1944, published in *The Irish Press*, caught in mid-air, his whole body bundled, his ribs tight, his arms ropy, the length of the canal dark behind him, the sky above him white, a look of fierce concentration on his face. The caption read, simply, *Boy above Canal*. His mother bought all the copies she could find in the small shop on Baggot Street Bridge. They have yellowed and even disintegrated now, but not the memory: it was her next door, quite literally, in the very next house—and she came across and slipped the newspaper clipping under the door. He watched her from the bay window. Eileen Daly. Even then she was a beauty. Alabaster skin and a row of dainty freckles paintbrushed across her nose. So beautiful in fact that he never talked to her at all in those years. Not once. Not even a glancing hello or goodbye or how are you Eileen Daly, isn't it a fine Dublin day? But he watched her from afar and she took his breath away. A hollowing-out of his stomach.

The day he left Dublin, oh, the day. It was bright and dappled, a surprise of sunshine. The hackney pulled up outside, a large silver car, an air horn on the side with a loud commanding blast. The bags were packed. The suitcases were loaded. He hid himself in the cupboard underneath the stairs. America. He didn't want to go. Didn't want to leave Ireland at all. But his father had a job offer. A letter had arrived. Elaborate handwriting. An eight-cent stamp with a picture of a twin-motored transport plane. An invitation, or maybe an accusation. Another continent. He was dragged out from underneath the stairs, shoved down the steps and into the waiting car. He glanced backwards through the rear window and there she was, Eileen Daly, all eleven years of her—or was she ten?—waving to him from the window of her living room. The white curtains bracketing her face. Her head slightly tilted. A few wisps of dark hair around her shoulders. Her lips pursed open ever so minutely, as if about to speak. He knew even then that he would see her this way forever, his mind had processed a photograph and seared itself on his brain. He wanted to turn to wave to her again, but the hackney had already reached the corner and he waved instead at a dirty brick wall.

Ireland.

Gone.

A chuisle mo chroí.

Whatever that means. Love of my heart or something like that. *Bubbala,* they might say in Yiddish. She had told him once and often, but it was a queer language, Irish, or Gaelic, he could never get the hang of it, it rolled marbles in his throat, the *dún an doras,* the *má sé do thoil é,* but the door was indeed shut, the sky went down and fell into the Irish Sea.

On the boat from Dun Laoghaire he heaved his guts up over the side and looked back towards the land until it became just the white of a wave. A miserable sunshine poured down upon him. He thought at least it could have had the dignity to rain one last time. Then, from Liverpool, they took off for America. The posh rooms. Port out, starboard home. He moped along the deck, Eileen Daly, Eileen Daly, Eileen Daly. Her name lay gentle on his tongue. He wasn't allowed into the ship's saloon, or even the library, but there was a billiard room by the first-class cabins where he sat in the corner and began writing her letters, his every waking moment consumed in the glance she gave him from the window. He couldn't understand how he had never said a word to her: what was it that had paralyzed him? They had lived next door to each other for the best part of two years and now here he was writing her page after page, telling her about the sunsets over the water, and the odd way the lifeboats creaked, and his glance back to Ireland, everything and anything, he wrote at a furious pace, head down, fountain pen gliding over the paper, he had never written so much in his life, eleven years old—or was he twelve?—didn't matter, he had the ancient disease, stupid, ridiculous, endless, it was his very first taste of what he would know later, intimately, wonderfully, the best of the four-letter words.

Eileen, I leaned, I lean.

Life is not so easy as to cross a field. Pasternak again. For sure this time, and oh, the mind is indeed a deep stone well, but how often a surprising bucket dips down into it and hits cool water. Eileen read the Russian poet's books aloud many nights, with her Irish lilt and a blanket pulled up around her neck, soft wool, Avoca, where the rivers met, or so she told him. She was a fount of Irish knowledge, and Russian knowledge, and even Jewish knowledge at times, a Helicon indeed, with some Greek thrown in and a smidge of Latin. Thankfully she never had to see me in the diaper, the nappy, the winter gear, down by those Salley gardens my love and I did meet.

He tilts his coffee cup and sighs. Empty now, just a small rivulet making its way along the inside of the porcelain. All life slowed down to this. The drip. The drop. The snow white feet.

Slowly falling, falling slowly. Out the window now. Big white flurries against the glass. That was a story she loved so much too, snow general all over Ireland, Michael Furey singing at the window, poor Gabriel left alone, the descent of his last end.

He tilts the coffee cup one last time and allows the last drop to fall on the newspaper where he watches it slowly blot and spread. *A bi gezunt,* his mother would have said. She was always one for the ancient phrase. You have your health, what more do you want?

—Sally?

He can hear her now in the kitchen, the rattle-out of the dishwasher, the clank along the rollers. Why in the world she needs to run the dishwasher he'll never know, it's not as if I spoiled a hundred plates with marmalade and toast.

And what is it that he wanted to say to Sally anyway, so deep in thought was he, back in Ireland, the good years, why interrupt them now, except perhaps the memory is so raw, and snow is general all over Eighty-sixth Street, the half-living, and I think she died for love, Eileen, I think she died for love.

—Mr. J.?

—It's snowing out there.

—Yes, Mr. J.

Looking at him now, expecting something else. Hardly enough to interrupt her from the dishwasher just to tell her what she already knows, the snow coming down like an argument for snow.

—I was just thinking, he says.

She nods and her gold earrings go jangling. Looking at him now very curiously. What is it that goes on in her head? Does she think I'm senile? All age and folly? An old white man in his old white body? Does she think of slaveships coming across the waves? Does she think of her own darling grandson back there in the Caribbean? Isn't that what she saves for? To send him to school? A good education for her grandson, or is it her nephew?

Kindhearted Sally, all her life directed towards that boy. Don't let him break your heart, Sally. And does she remember the good days I had with Eileen? Does she recall the fine household we had? Though truth be told, they sometimes went at it hammer and tongs, Sally and Eileen, many a good argument indeed, black and white, and Eileen had a sharp tongue on her, she could sometimes cut Sally down, the big tall tree tumbling, and oh, what is it I wanted to say, what did I need?

—I think I'd like to go to Chialli's today, Sally.

His almost daily ritual.

—Yes, sir. In the snow?

—In the snow, yes, ma'am.

—You made you a reservation?

He scoots backwards in his chair. I do indeed have a reservation, Sally, though truth be told it's more with your grammar, not the restaurant. Hardly worth it to correct her now, let bygods be bygones.

—What time is it, Sally?

—Ten fifteen, sir.

—Let's make one for one.

—Sir?

—One o'clock, Sally. Call Chialli's. And I'll call Elliot. Maybe he can drag himself away for once.

She is lovely, once and always, Sally James, moonlight in her hair, wherever she walks cool breezes fan the glade, I strolled with her beneath the leafy shade, oh, I never kissed a black woman in my life, but it must be said that many of them have beautiful lips, and teeth to match, but not Sally, more's the pity, or maybe just as well, no ancient temptations. Still and all, the old songs are always the best.

—Yes, sir, Mr. J.

—Thank you, Sally.

One never forgets the first kiss though, and while there were a few before Eileen—some that were paid for, if truth be told, in Dresden, the shiksas along the barrack walls who were known for their questionable virginity—it was really just all Eileen, and even if she wasn't the first, she was, she always would be, now and tomorrow and the day after. How many letters did he send to her over the years? Hundreds, thousands even. Eileen Daily, she once called herself. Lovely once and always, with moonlight in her hair. He wrote to her from his high school in the Bronx. He wrote to her from the corridors of Fordham. He wrote to her when he joined the Air Force. And all that time he had never even said a single word to her, face-to-face. How odd it was to know someone so well and never have talked a single word in her presence. There was, of course, the telephone, and they had chatted down the wires, perplexed by one another's accents, but never face-to-face, and it was not until 1952 when he was stationed in Dresden, an office job, checking flight patterns, an awful bore, day in, day out, reams of paperwork, clouds of pipesmoke, but he still wrote two letters a day, and she wrote back to him, grand professions of love and literature, and then he had a week of R & R, and he shined his shoes, pomaded his hair, stepped aboard a plane to Glasgow, where he hired a car, and met her in Edinburgh where she was studying literature, and neither of them could ever remember the very first words they spoke to each other, quite possibly they were speechless, but later that night he fell to his knees and asked her to marry him, you're the love of my life, *a chuisle mo chroí,* you wrote it to me in several of your letters, I don't know quite what it means, but marry me, please, Eileen, do. She blushed and said yes, and she lowered her eyelids, and his heart hammered in his shirt, and he said it would be a stylish marriage, though if we're telling the truth, the whole truth, and nothing but the truth, it must be said that very little is ever truly idyllic, except in retrospect, and, to be honest now, he was just a tiny bit disappointed by Eileen Daly when he saw her first, she was not quite how he remembered her, at the window, in Leeson Street, looking out, raindrops across her eyes, no, she had grown a tad pudgier and her skin was of a pallor that tended away from the pink he remembered, and she was rather ordinary of eye-color, though he soon forgot that, and she became lovely again, if not even lovelier, but if another truth be told—a deeper truth—he was hardly a perfect specimen himself, rather he was a long thin drink of water with a big pair of spectacles on his nose, and anxious eyes, and his trousers at half-mast as if his own body was in mourning for what God gave him, and a skinny set of arms on him, not exactly a nautilus man, he couldn't afford a carriage, a few stray hairs on his chin, already the fuzz on the dome thinning, a little peninsula on top of his head, and truly he had to admit that, later that night, when he tucked himself into bed next door, that he was getting the better end of the deal, marrying Eileen Mendelssohn, née Daly, and they fit rather well together, hand in hand along Anne Street, the whole world open to them, they would be married in six months and living in New York where she tested her new name on her tongue, and wandered along the Avenue of the Americas in full and righteous bloom, oh, she loved Leopold Bloom, too, that's for sure, and where in the world did I come up with that phrase *questionable virginity*?

Which reminds me, I must call my errant son.

Where in the world, Sally, did I put my BlackBerry? Is it here, beneath the newspaper, everything that's fit to print, anchored down by my empty coffee cup?

Oh, Eileen, I miss you. Daily, daily, daily.

V

I do not know which to prefer,
The beauty of inflections
Or the beauty of innuendos,
The blackbird whistling
Or just after.

Poets, like detectives, know the truth is laborious: it doesn't occur by accident, rather it is chiseled and worked into being, the product of time and distance and graft. The poet must be open to the possibility that she has to go a long way before a word rises, or a sentence holds, or a rhythm opens, and even then nothing is assured, not even the words that have staked their original claim or meaning. Sometimes it happens at the most unexpected moment, and the poet has to enter the mystery, rebuild the poem from there.

There are thirty-four days of footage from each of the eight cameras in Mendelssohn's building: 59 East Eighty-sixth Street, between Madison and Park Avenues, just two hundred yards from the restaurant. The first camera captures the double glass doorways of the pre-war building, the high steps, the awning. The picture widens to the far sidewalk, the north side of Eighty-sixth Street. A limited angle, poor depth of field, north to south, recorded with a 50 mm lens. Another in the lobby itself. One in the laundry room downstairs. One on the staircase. One on the roof. One in the elevator. One by the boiler room. Another in the storage area downstairs.

On the afternoon of his death, Mendelssohn emerges from the elevator—an uneventful ride, he stands silently alongside Sally James—and they walk together into the lobby.

It is one of those ancient New York foyers, marble and flowers and chandeliers. Brass wall lights. A mahogany table. Black-and-white tiles. A long strip of carpet down the middle. Bad art on the walls, the sort created expressly not to offend.

Sally disappears around the corner a moment, and Mendelssohn takes a few steps alone. He wears a long overcoat. A Homburg hat. A drowsy determination on his face. The space awaiting his chronic fate. In zoom the eyes are hooded, the jaw is slack, he wears little half-moons of fatigue beneath his spectacles. A burst of wrinkles from the eyes. Another little burst of hair from the side of his hat. His head deeply veined at the side temples. The small sag of skin and the chickenwattle at his neck. The marks of decades. The detectives can imagine him at home, slackmouthed in sleep, his pajama collar askew, a light snore sailing from the back of his throat.

But later, when he moves along the corridor, they notice a drop of joy in his shuffle. Not a sideways lean or a bedraggled pull-along. A man still attached to the world. A curmudgeonly grace. The detectives examine the walk, as if the movement might carry a forensic clue to his being. They are well aware that a moment on its own, like a word, means little or nothing, but it is their accumulation that begins to make them matter. Life has been made strange by a series of actions and so there must be a corresponding series of triggers. The past is a key to the future: hidden causes must become plain, time should move to a singular point of revelation. The thrill is in finding the point where the mystery is dismantled. Then they can jigsaw the logic back together. If they can find one piece, they will glimpse another nearby, test it for fit.

The trick eventually comes in the agility to see the pieces all at once, and then build outward and backward—to commit the solution.

On the strength of the fluidity of motion alone, simply the way he walks, the detectives are sure that there has been no death threat to Mendelssohn, no advance suggestion of murder, even when he raps his walking stick on the ground and Sally James rounds the corner from the elevator, and seems to put a hand to his throat. His neck looks wattled and slack, as if it might be about to sound out the after-gulps of a sink. But then she gently wraps the scarf around him, and moves forward, supporting his elbow.

The nurse is, by all appearances, well looked after. She wears a large coat with fur on the collar. On her feet, tall boots.

They shuffle the length of the corridor and stand inside the double front doors. Sally pauses and turns while Mendelssohn has a word with the doorman, Tony DiSalvo, a man who looks lifted from a Mexican cantina, portly and balding, a hint of violence about him and yet a suggestion, also, of rumbling intelligence. Later, under questioning, it will be revealed that Tony is Puerto Rican, a former philosophy major from the University of Miami, but that the conversation was just yet another of those daily New York exchanges about the weather, how awful it is outside, how much snow there has been this winter, a familiar joke from Mendelssohn about being out to lunch, and how Tony wants Mendelssohn to be careful at the traffic lights, the taxis have been sliding all morning long.

Tony helps Mendelssohn down the steep steps and watches as the old man and the nurse step out of frame.

The detectives scrub through the footage from the previous days too, in case they can find something in the patterns of time that will propel them toward a critical epiphany, a mid-verse logic. A meter. An enjambment. Or a rhyme.

For the week of the murder they watch at a rate of thirty-two by: the world zooming past. A whole day slips along in less than an hour. There is a comic texture to the motion, especially when Mendelssohn, with his nurse, uses his cane and stutterstarts out of the frame. As the days wind down, they slow the picture and go forward at a rate of sixteen by, then eight by. Each minute takes seven and a half seconds. Four hours in half an hour. Their fingers glide over the keys. Looking. Digging. Scratching. Mining. A face seen one two three times. Someone loitering near the awning. A covert glance. A nervous tic. Or maybe something more brazen, more obvious, an assailant with a malevolent fuck-you stare. Every incident with its own peculiar rhythm: the ordinary comings, the goings, the delivery trucks, the doorman shuffle, the tenants, Mendelssohn and his nurse, the arrival of the snowstorm.

On the day of the murder they watch in real time, stopping, starting, chopping, rewinding. Over and over again. Think. Stop. Rethink. Watch Mendelssohn emerge. Gaze at the storm. Adjust his collar. Kick the first of the white snow off his shoe. Lean against his nurse. See Sally laugh. See Tony nod. See Mendelssohn smile. See nothing odd. See Mendelssohn go. See the old man disappear. See the snow coming down.

They wait, careful with the time stamp, to discover if anything happens in the intervening hour, but it is only the doorway, the awning, the pavement, the street, the increasing white of the storm, the return, back into frame, of Sally from the restaurant, with a nod to Tony and a blow of warm air into her hands, little else. For a while they wait for Mendelssohn to return from lunch, as if the video itself could trump reality.

They scrub the footage forward a few hours, just in case: a murderer is often known to return to the site of his work. They scan the faces of neighbors, paramedics, delivery boys, voyeurs, all hanging around the front entrance of the apartment building. The detectives dig through the ordinary, looking for any tiny finger-smear of evidence, any face that pops, a shadow that threatens. The evidence could be there in the oddest of moments, the briefest of glances, the slightest of shoulder rubs. They focus in on the son, Elliot Mendelssohn, the hedge fund man, political aspirant, well-known philanderer, parting the crowd. He is tall and broad-shouldered, with a large stomach, as if he has swallowed a bag of rocks. In and out of the building Elliot goes, several times, a cell phone clutched to his ear, a harried look on his face as if he might never have the chance to talk to anyone more interesting than himself.

Late in the evening Elliot emerges with a torn black ribbon placed over his heart, and the detectives, with their radar for the unusual, find it interesting that he could have so early a showcase of grief especially given the secular nature of the Mendelssohns: did he have the ribbon stored in his jacket beforehand? Did he tear one upstairs in his father's apartment?

Later they observe the arrival of nephews and cousins and in-laws and old friends to the apartment: nothing creates a family quite like a murder.

The detectives slide back on the digital timeline to the moment when Mendelssohn steps out into the snowstorm: there is something of the Greek epic about it, the old gray man with his walking stick, venturing out, into the snow, out of frame and away, like an ancient word stepping off a page.

VI

Icicles filled the long window
With barbaric glass.
The shadow of the blackbird
Crossed it, to and fro.
The mood
Traced in the shadow
An indecipherable cause.

Trusty walking stick. Old reliable. He could, of course, use the Zimmerframe or even the motorized wheelchair upstairs, collecting dust in the rear bedroom, but why draw attention? He'd rather not end up like all those idiots zipping along Fifth Avenue, beep beep, out of the way, colonoscopy call, Fifth Avenue here I come, pave the way, Dr. Jim. He had to use a chair once, a few years ago, when he broke his hip after a tumble outside the Guggenheim. On a patch of ice. Before he knew it, he was sprawled on the pavement. The management was scared that he might sue, but that was not his style, he loved the law, respected it, obeyed it. It wasn't for trifling idiocies like an old man's fall. Two weeks in the hospital and then Elliot bought him a motorized chair. More buttons on it than an SOC-3. Magnetos engaged. Radar on. Spin that propeller. Contact! He crashed it into the hospital bed on his very first try. You needed a PhD in civil engineering just to sit in the thing for crying out loud.

Come on now, Sally.

Enough chitchat.

There she is, around the corner, at the daily conference of the housekeeping brigade. The Help, some people say. What a terrible thing to call them, but what other word is there? Not servants. Not domestics. Not aides, God forbid, they're no disease. They congregate down by the mailboxes. One of them, he knows, is Russian. Another Welsh. Another Slovakian. Their own little United Nations in the lobby. He has often wondered what sort of chinwaggery goes on down there, who pays what, and who shouted at whom, and who got fired when, and why. The Yenta Brigade. All the gossip that's fit to print. Every building in the city like a village in itself. The penthouse, the castle. The corridors, the streets. The stairwell, the alleyways. The elevator, the main thoroughfare. The storage space, the dump. The boiler room, the factory. The handyman, the cobbler. The doormen, the police. The super, the judge. And the judge himself, well, he's the village putz, left waiting in the lobby, waiting, waiting.

He raps his walking stick on the marble floor. Once. Twice.

They're gossiping still around the corner. A high laugh and then a low whisper and then another cackle from Sally herself. What was it like in the Garden of Eden before there was a snake? No wonder Adam went for the apple. Or was it Eve who ate the apple? Strange how the simplest things slip from our minds. The original tale, and he can't even recall who it was that transgressed. Or maybe nobody transgressed at all. Maybe they bit the apple together. Shared it. And why not? There was an old rhyme he knew as a ten-year-old: *Wouldn't it have been jolly if Eve's leaf had been holly?* What a marvelous thing, a woman's body. Curved and designed for delight. Full and glorious and open for invitation, invocation, inhalation. Lord, he loved lying with Eileen on a Sunday morning, especially after high-jinks if they got the chance. They would watch the light crawl into the room, beckon it, good days, the horn of plenty, so to speak, once upon a time.

He hits his walking stick on the floor once more. Oh, come on now, Sally. Lord above. Onwards. Old men grow older quicker. Sally up, Sally forth, Sally sixth.

—Right there, Mr. J.

—I haven't got all day, you know.

She pops her head around the corner.

—Right with you, Mr. J.

And then he hears a complicated sigh. And a giggle.

I hope to God that she isn't telling them about my adventures in the diaper trade. You work your whole life to become a pillar of the community and then it all disappears in front of your eyes.

Perhaps he should just strike out into the snow on his own. Hand me my oxygen tank. Pull my hat down around my ears. Sir Edmund, hitting the slopes. Once he climbed the mountains in Italy with Eileen. Up in the beautiful Dolomites. They stayed in a chalet under the shadows of the mountains and in the mornings, after breakfast, they climbed up through the spectacular forests, hand in hand, and then used carabiners to clip themselves in to scale the *via ferrate*, high into the sky. The amazing thing about the Italians was that they had *rifugios* on the top of the mountains. You could eat a bowl of pasta and drink a glass of pinot grigio twelve thousand feet in the air. A civilized bunch. He often wishes that he had a little of the Italian blood in him, that big expansive generosity, that color, that style, but it's all Lithuanian, which, of course, is its own little mishmash, Polish and Russian and German and Viking too.

Curious thing, the blood we inherit. Slapping around inside, making us who we are: the landscape itself gets a say in the outcome of the mind. Tobago with its beaches and sunlight and palm trees, no doubt, where life is designed to slow things down. Still, Sally somehow gets things done, it always amazes him at the end of the day the place is clean, the laundry is folded, the dishes are washed, the beds are tucked, and she disappears to her little room, where she keeps a picture of her nephew, or her grandson, on the table, and once or twice he has heard her weeping, but most of the time she goes happily off to sleep, or so it seems. Oh, nature's soft nurse, how I have frighted thee.

Still and all, he wishes she would get a move on. He gazes the length of the lobby towards the snow falling white and fat-flaked outside. Strange how life becomes a telescope: the distance lengthening the older we get. He has lived in this building the best part of twenty years and the lobby has never been longer. He raises a salutary finger to Tony the doorman who is outside sprinkling rock salt on the ground. He has known Tony for two decades now. Seen him age and bloom and indeed balloon. Time. The great leveler. Since when did Tony suddenly hit the far side of middle age? It's not as if this sort of thing happens overnight, or is it? Found him once reading a copy of Kant. Tried to make a joke. *I tried Kant, but couldn't.* Fell flat. To Tony anyway. Which I might well do right now. Flat on my face in the lobby, waiting. Come on, Sally, for crying out loud.

There was a while in his own life, in his late thirties, when everything just fell away so suddenly: the hair, the ease, the grace. Walked around with a big lump of anxiety in his heart. A midlife crisis they called it. Didn't begin to feel reinvigorated, really, until he reached the age of fifty. Elected, then, to Supreme Court, Kings County. Hardly a runaway election, but the party backed him, they even made him little buttons and leaflets to hand out at the polling stations around Brooklyn. Truth was they needed a liberal Jew and he just about fit the bill. They liked his Catholic wife as well, two birds with one poll. They lived in the Heights, so they had the cachet. Dugan Brothers Bakery Delivered to Your Door. He walked every day to the courts on Adams Street. The great thing about being a justice of the court was that you didn't have to retire until seventy, seventy-six if you pushed it. It was written there under Judiciary Law, three two-year extensions. Sure, they put the thumbscrews on and the inevitable hints were dropped, especially because he moved to Manhattan—he was no longer their Brooklyn boy, how dare he move to the city?—but he hung in there until the end, especially after Eileen left, oh Lord, the day. He was in the bathroom on Eighty-sixth Street having a shave, half his face covered in foam, when he heard the thumping fall outside the door. She'd been sick for a long time but he had no idea that she was going to pass just like that—a quick fall as she stepped out of bed—and there she was, Eileen, lying on the carpet, gone, gone, *a chuisle mo chroí*. He leaned down and stroked her hair. That's what he would remember, the feel of her hair. They say that it's one of the last things to go. That it keeps on growing. Even days after. That's why they have to shave the dead.

—Isn't that right, Sally?

She has come, at last, around the corner, the little hem of her nurse whites showing beneath the dark of her coat.

—What's that Mr. J.?

—I was just thinking—

—Yes? she says with a swell of boredom. She reaches up and adjusts his scarf tight around his neck.

—About Mrs. Mendelssohn.

—Yes, sir, Mr. J., sir. A fine woman, Miss Eileen.

—I do, I do.

—Excuse me, sir?

—Oh, don't worry about me, Sally.

—On you go, Mr. J., I got you.

The dead are with us. They glide along behind us on our endless journeys, they accompany us in our smallest gestures, tuck themselves into our dark shadows, they even come along on our little lunchtime sojourns to Chialli's. She used to comb her hair with a gold-handled brush. He loved watching her by the mirror, the stroke of the brush and the fan of her hair, pressing the long strands together with thumb and forefinger.

—Lovely once and always.

—Mr. J.?

—It's an old tune.

—Yes, sir. Of course.

—Lovely once and always, moonlight in her hair.

—Yes, sir.

Sally is of course quite thoroughly confused, but how could she have any idea in heaven or hell what he's talking about, unless the song got diverted and made it all the way to Tobago. And damn it all anyway. He can feel a little tremor in his pocket but he's not about to stop out here, now, in the lobby, no matter who's calling, God or Elliot or Job or anyone else for that matter. How odd to get that little vibration down below. A wocket in my pocket. He used to read Dr. Seuss to Katya long ago. They were good days, reading to the children when he had the time. Odd thing, time. So much of it now and we spend it all looking back. Lovely once and always with moonlight in her hair.

—Lord above, says Sally, looking out to the weather. You sure you want to venture out, Mr. J.?

He loves this, too, about Sally, the way every now and then she will burst forth with a word that he doesn't expect. *Venture* indeed. Add venture, dear Sally. Upwards. Away.

He pauses on the lip of the first glass door, at the steps. A cold blast of air hits him as Tony hurries in to help.

—Young man.

—How are we today, Mr. Mendelssohn?

—Out to lunch.

His old joke. Guaranteed to bring a smile to Tony's lips. It's the repetition that makes it funnier: he says it almost every single day, rain, hail, shine. What would happen, one fine day, if he didn't say it at all? The world would hardly stop spinning, but it might just hiccup a little on its axis. We Kan, we Kant.

—And who's this lovely lady?

Tony the charmer. A beam from Sally. Yes, indeed, he loves that smile. It's a good world, this, in its odd little moments.

—We just got married in the elevator, didn't we, Sally?

—Yes, sir, we did.

—Hope you picked up all the confetti.

—Check the recycle bin.

—You're very considerate, Mr. Mendelssohn.

It's a high step down from the lobby into the street and getting higher every day. Feels like I'm lowering myself from a crane. Into the recyclables indeed. Maybe Katya and Elliot should hang handles along the length of Eighty-sixth Street: from the streetlamps, swinging along, like Johnny Weissmuller through the jungle, here we come.

—Careful now, says Tony. Can't have the newlyweds crash.

There is still only a light dusting on the ground, but the storm is gathering force. Best get out and about now, quick and early. Who knows how long he might be housebound if it truly comes tumbling down?

He places the walking stick firmly on the ground, bends his weight into the leg. The creak of the knee. The rumble of the ankle. Here we go. Thank you, Sally. Doing just fine on my own.

Curious thing, the snow. They say the Eskimos have eighty words for it. An articulate lot. Slush and sleet and firn and grain. Hoar and rime. Crust crystal vapor blizzard graupel. Pendular permeable planar. Striated shear supercooled. Brittle glazed clustered coarse broken. An insult of snow, a slur of snow, a taunt of snow, a Walt Whitman snow, a bestiary snow, a calliope snow, it's snowing in Morse code, three longs, a short, a long again, it's snowing like the ancient art of the newspaper, it's snowing like September dust coming down, it's snowing like a Yankees Day parade, it's snowing like an Eskimo song.

One step two steps three steps five. He stops for a moment at a muni-meter. God be with the days when you could park your carcass for a nickel, what do they cost now, two dollars for ten minutes, less, more? He watches a bus going past, chains on the tires. A woman on a bicycle. Good balance that. The shadow of death crossing to and fro. Careful, young lady. A minivan, beeping its way through the snow, perilously close to the cyclist.

The flashers flashing. The horn blaring. Good God, don't hit her. Oh.

—That was close, Sally.

The hair on her chinny-chin-chin.

—Uh-huhn.

Sally too. There's a market for that: a razor for elderly ladies. Eileen never had that problem. Smooth as silk.

He touches his hat and shuffles on. The trusty walking stick needed more than ever. A steel tip on the end. No sound from it today. Muffled.

—I'm building up an appetite, Sally.

—Yes, sir.

He pauses by the fire hydrant, to gather his breath. Can never see a fire hydrant without thinking of the September dust coming down ten years ago. All those young firemen going up the stairs. All intimately connected. A terrible day, he watched the collapse on television. For weeks afterwards every little thing was charged with meaning, even the dust on the windowsill, you were never quite sure what it might contain: a paper, a résumé, an eyelash.

—Sally, my dear, you are an angel.

—You're out of breath, Mr. J.

—Just pretending, Sally.

He stands at the edge of the crosswalk. Why is it that the traffic lights are designed to humiliate us? Once he could get across from one side to the other without the little neon man flashing at all. These days he can only get halfway before the red man starts his antics. There is nothing he hates more than when the cars start to inch forward. Mendelssohn, your time is up. Goodbye, thank you, now sidle off to Florida. Or North Carolina. Down there the neon man lasts infinitely longer. It's a known fact.

Here they go already, hooting and tooting. It never ceases to amaze him, how downright rude the city can be. Eight million lives colliding all at once. All those tiny little atoms in the process of bouncing off each other. Yes, yes, lady, you will have a chance to move your tush, but please just hush, and give me a chance to move my own.

One of the things he used to love about New York City was the sheer bravado of it all. It used you up, spat you out. But the more the years went on, the more he began to think that he'd like a little respect from it. He had, after all, put his time in. Sat on the bench. Went to party meetings. A Supreme Court justice. A fancy title, but in reality he got every case under the Brooklyn sun, a clearing house, really, for murders, mobsters, shysters, shucksters. The random stabbings. The premeditated take-downs. Probate matters. Injunctions. Rescissions. An endless ream of paperwork. He stayed within the system even at the worst of times. Never strayed. At half the salary he would have made if he had gone into corporate law. After all that he would have liked just a little ripple of thanks from the peanut gallery. A moment longer in the crosswalk, please. He put his career as a lawyer in the bin for a life of public service, and what did he get? Some fresh young tchotchke in a black SUV with New Jersey license plates looking as if she'd like nothing more than to flatten him in one fell swoop. Windshield wipers slapping back and forth. Her petulant glare. Her lip gloss shining. An ex-Juicy.

Drumming her fingers on the steering wheel. Don't think I don't see you, young lady. Just because I'm going along here slow as molasses doesn't mean that I'm not aware that you would very much like to put the pedal to the metal, scoop up poor Sally in the process, and drag us along Eighty-sixth Street, hanging to your bumper. A bit of respect, please. Objection sustained. There was a case he handled once of a kid from Bed-Stuy who was tied to the back of a garbage truck and dragged through the streets, he had been left lying on the ground for two hours afterwards, all the evidence was there but the jury wouldn't convict. Rephrase. Move on. It was hard to leave a case like that behind. Haunted him for years. A young black boy, skidding along. Brutal days.

Who in the world designed those SUVs anyway? The ugliest damn things on the face of the earth. A big silver grille and a ram on the hood. As if they're heading off to war. And why in the world are they needed anyway? It's not as if she's heading across the Rockies, flooding rivers and endless jungle.

—It's always Jersey, Sally.

—Sir?

—It's always a Jersey license plate.

—You take your sweet time, Mr. J. Don't mind her. We can stay here until Sunday if we want.

—We might get snowed in.

How many mornings, noons, and nights have I walked up and down this street? How many footsteps along this same path? When I was young and nimble and slick I would dart across the

road in the Dublin traffic, horse carriages, bicycles, milktrucks
and all. Jaywalking. Jayshuffling it is, now. The jaybird. Mr. J.,
indeed. On the Upper East Side. A lot of volume in this life.
Echoes too.

—Just fine.

Sally's hand lies steady on his elbow now. Gripping rather
hard into what is left of the muscle. The walking stick in his
other hand, propping him up and propelling him along. And
why is it that the mind can do anything it wants, yet the body
won't follow? What a wonderful thing it would be to live as a
brain for a little while. To be perched in a jar and see it all from
there. Without the rigors of the meshuggeneh mansion? A pure
clean life. On a shelf. In a row of shelves. Not stuck out here,
shambling in the snow, watching the red man flash and the New
Jersey lady fume, and listening to her horn beep, and the whole
of New York City build up behind her.

—All right, lady, all right.

—Shut up! says Sally with a glare.

The woman yanks the steering wheel hard and then pulls out
around him. The tires spin in the light crust of snow. Time nor
tide wait for no woman. Especially if she's from Trenton. Or
Wayne. Or worse yet, Newark. Good God, but she's in a rush.

Maybe off for a dalliance somewhere who knows, maybe
even a tryst with his very own Elliot. How come that boy never
learned to keep his equipment in his trousers?

The red man is static now. Not even flashing. A Geronimo of
the avenue. Wasn't the neon sign a different color back once,

long ago? Wasn't there a large neon hand once? Or is there still? There most certainly was a *Walk, Don't Walk*. It was so very New York, the insistence of it, the brash instruction. Walk or else. There was another sign also: *Don't Even Think of Parking Here*. And once, long ago, he saw a sign in Hell's Kitchen that said: *Park Here, Motherfucker, and You Will*. Which was funny, even if grammatically unsound. Park here and you will park here? Or park here and you will fuck your mother? Or both? Or neither? Or something in between?

Oh, no matter, Your Honor. Just get across the street. All Wimbledon rules have been suspended.

Another loud beeping. The traffic on the far side of Eighty-sixth has begun to move towards him. A Sikh in a taxi. Hold your turbines, sir. Good God, a pull of pain through his knees. A fierce tightness in the shoulders. His hips feel as if they've been lowered down into cement. We were young once, Sally. It's like crossing the Styx.

One foot after the next. That's all you should think about. One step at a time. Like an Alcoholics Anonymous for geriatrics. Another curb. Borrow the crane. Avoid the grates at all costs. Don't get stuck in the Styx.

And hallelujah, thank the heavens, he gets to the edge of the curb and stabilizes himself against Sally. Both of them breathing a little heavily now.

—They're even worse if they're Chinese.

—Hhhhrrrummmpf, she says.

—It's a well-known fact. The Chinese have the worst driving records. I don't know why. They're good people but they damn sure can't drive.

—Is that so?

—If you ever meet a Chinese man from New Jersey, buckle up.

—You're funny, Mr. J.

Which, quite plainly, he is not. She doesn't even have the faintest of smiles. Out here, shivering. She's not used to it at all. A couple of decades in New York and still she has the Caribbean sunshine in her bones. He should invite her to lunch. Always, every day, she accompanies him, and he brings her home some of Dandinho's specially wrapped leftovers. She loves them. Twists them open. Puts the food on a plate. Microwaves it. Sits and watches soap operas on her little TV through the night. A tough life she has, Sally James. He would love, now, to see one of her enormous smiles. Something to crack open the day and whisk away the cold. But she's intent on getting him down the road and squared away for his lunchtime ritual.

—On we go.

Moving like a tugboat. The flower shop, the chocolatier, the perfumery, the antique store, the wine shop, the handbag seller, the dry cleaners: everything the modern human needs.

Roll up, roll up. The shutters of life.

Hardly any pedestrians on the street today. A few delivery boys and a couple of hurrying mothers with their prams. One brave jogger wearing shorts, bouncing down the avenue like it's August. Never understood that jogging phenomenon. Chest hair and headbands. Sometimes both at once. Snow in August. A good man wrote a book with that same title, what's his name, he edited the newspaper once, was in love with Jackie O, so the rumor went anyway, or rather was she in love with him?

Sally on one side, the walking stick on the other. The hat on my head. The overcoat nice and toasty. The stomach rumbling and ready. What more could a man want? Eileen, Eileen, Eileen.

And I hate that, I truly do. Those hidden hats of dogshit left sprinkled on the sidewalk. Like little sombreros. Always in wintertime as well. A disgrace. All it takes is a doggie bag and a gentle scoop. Off with the sombrero and into the trash.

Land ahoy. The brown-and-orange awning. The large plate-glass windows. The beautifully scripted writing in the window. The small pleated curtains. The glow of round lamps. A home away from home. Pete Hamill, that's the man.

—Careful now, Mr. J. Watch your step.

They pause a moment outside the handbag shop, and he leans towards her, sees a snowflake perch on her long eyelash.

—What time'll I pick you up, Mr. J.?

—Elliot will walk back with me.

—You sure?

—Sure, I'm sure.

—Sure sure?

—I'm sure, Sally.

How many *sure*s in a row? Love loves to love love. The little snowflake perched there on the ledge of her lash. Beauty comes and beauty goes.

—You know, I've never asked you, Sally.

—Sir?

—Which do you prefer? Salmon or steak?

She blinks and the snowflake is gone. Eyelashes. Towers. And why is it he always just brings her the leftovers anyway? Why is it that she gets the dregs of the day, the diapers too? He should buy her a whole plate and get it specially wrapped by Dandinho. Or even better, dress her up, take her out, celebrate her, she's a good soul, Sally James, looking after her fine young nephew down there in Scarborough if I'm not mistaken, ah, the mind returns, yes, Tobago for sure, not Trinidad.

—Oh, don't you worry about me, Mr. J., she says. I'm just fine.

—A little brownie perhaps?

—You're sweet, Mr. J.

And she kisses him on the cold of his cheek.

VII

O thin men of Haddam,
Why do you imagine golden birds?
Do you not see how the blackbird
Walks around the feet
Of the women about you?

The household fly is a masterpiece of evolutionary design: it can see virtually 360 degrees and can piece together a complete image no matter how weak the light. Its compound eye is an intricate honeycomb. Its retina is a convex curve, dotted with hundreds of hexagonal photoreceptors. Each lens of the eye—with support cells, pigment cells, a cornea—harvests its own light and creates a deep visual map.

The fly can spot movement in shadows, and can pick out distant objects with far more clarity than anything the human can accomplish. The result is a mosaic of light, color, pattern, and speed. The images the fly sees are smashed together in its brain. The more lenses used, the higher the resolution.

On a microscopic slide, the insect's eye looks like an exquisite artwork, the tiling on the wall of a mosque, or the curve of a planet we haven't yet found.

With the eye of a simple housefly we could see, in a nanosecond, all the intricacies of Chialli's Restaurant, the tables arranged in diamonds, the door opening on the walk-in fridge, the frantic slice of the knife upon the carrot, the creased folds of the napkins, the busboy adjusting the crank on the espresso machine, the manager turning to the wall for a sly crotch adjust, the slide of the bread basket on the food-station trays, the hostess touching a pencil against her tongue, the clearing of the dead man's plates from the table, the leap of hot oil from a pan.

As it is, there are twelve cameras in Chialli's altogether, neatly hidden in corners around the restaurant. A two-year-old system with a sixteen-camera capability, ports still open for four. Updated software with one terabyte of storage. Good compression, resolution and a full-motion frame rate with thirty images per second. The sort of system that is good enough that the video technicians can pump it to a remote location and examine it off-site.

It is a well-known restaurant, highly rated, very Upper East Side. A long mahogany bar. Dark wood paneling along the walls. A hardwood floor. A series of stained glass—shaded lights hanging from the ceiling over the tables. The restaurant is known for its Italian cuisine with a surprising South American flavor. The wine list is extensive. The service, impeccable. The speciality of the house is branzino, lightly grilled with mango and peppers. The most popular dessert is tiramisu, prepared with a hint of cachaça. The lunchtime crowd is generally quiet, well-heeled: the ladies who lunch.

The digital detectives exit the twelve-camera matrix and click on the images one by one: the kitchen, the manager's office, the hostess station, the dining room, the staff cloakroom, the rear courtyard. They layer them, bookend them, break them apart, look for tiny inconsistencies. Check the time stamps for offset. Zoom in, zoom out, build a dossier for themselves, examining the time close to the murder, 2:19 p.m., searching for anything out of the ordinary.

There, the coat-check girl, Laura Pedersen, with her book of tickets. There, the oyster shucker, Carvahlo, sharpening his knife. Here, the chef, Chad MacKenzie, adjusting his hair under his tall white hat. There, the manager, Christopher Eagleton, flipping through pages on a clipboard. There, Pedro Jiménez at the dishwashing station. Here, the dropped fork on the kitchen floor. There, the swing of the restaurant doors. Here, the busboy, Dandinho, guiding Mendelssohn to the table. There, Mendelssohn, wiping the napkin against his lip. Here, Elliot calmly sipping his Cabernet. There, the last glass of Sancerre that Mendelssohn ever drank. Here, the waitress, Rosita Oosterhausen, tapping orders on a keyboard and later pinching her nipple through her blouse seconds before she delivers the check, a tried and trusted way to increase tips.

There is a sequence, too, of the outer foyer of Chialli's, from Mendelssohn's arrival to the tail end of his goodbye.

There are a number of people to mark—not least Elliot Mendelssohn. He arrives late, big and bundled, in an overcoat and scarf. They watch him and his father dine at a rate of eight-by—the dab of napkins, the quick lift of fork to mouth, the pour of wine, no obvious arguments. They slow the video sequence down for Elliot's casual stroll toward the front doors, the donning of his wool hat, his walk out into the snowstorm, still nothing overtly suspicious about him, no signal, no nod, no wink. He leaves at 1:52, twenty-seven minutes before the murder. Still, so many killings are arranged by family members and the detectives cannot rule out an accomplice: there is something about Elliot that is distinctly unlikeable, not least his insistence on speaking on the phone during large portions of lunch.

Then there is Pedro Jiménez who is absent from his dishwashing station for a full four minutes before the murder and five minutes afterward. Pedro, fifty-seven, has no record, no violent past. At 2:12 they watch him and the busboy, Dandinho, in animated discussion by the giant metal sink under the Brooklyn Cyclones poster. It is interesting to watch Pedro remove his apron and throw it on the ground, and to see Dandinho hold him by the shoulders. There is a short pushing match between the two men. Later when they are questioned, it is revealed that Dandinho is Brazilian, and Pedro is Costa Rican, and they have a South American soccer betting pool where some mistakes have been made in the general accountancy. Pedro tells them that he was in the bathroom at the time of the murder. There are, of course, no bathroom cameras, but they do catch footage of him moving down the corridor in the direction of the toilets, a plausible-enough alibi.

Sally James, too, is tagged, though only half-heartedly. They scrub backward on the video timeline to the early angle outside Chialli's. They watch the dead man, alive, with Sally at his side. A shuffle to his walk, a distrust of the small coating of snow on the ground. The halting steps of one who refuses to tumble. The bite of wind active in his face. His body a little elongated from the angle. They enter the frame, actor-like, hitting their marks. The detectives halt the image and magnify, hold them in digital suspension, then click a slow motion forward. The pair hover at the entrance. She kisses him on the cheek, then Mendelssohn lets go of his nurse's arm, shuffles forward, slope-shouldered, and stops at the restaurant door. A single flake briefly obscures him when blown against the screen.

The detectives make a note to check if Mendelssohn's will has been recently changed, a not uncommon occurrence amongst nurses or housekeepers and their charges, though Sally James hardly seems the type.

It is what the cops call a shrapnel case—the pieces exploding left right center up and down. Could be mistaken identity. Could be a hate crime. There is also of course the possibility of the random psychotic episode: a homeless man thrown slightly off-kilter, or a desperate robber at large. But there is no wallet taken, no cell phone swiped. The point for the detectives is to find the focus, the muscles that have propelled the punch. Then they might be able to move it backward, through the ligaments to the bone and bring it back eventually to the raw moment of release.

Several theories are always less convincing than a single one, so for their primary one they remain with Elliot—there is certainly something there, though they cannot locate it yet: certainly it wouldn't be unusual for the son to murder the father, it happens far more often than anyone acknowledges.

After Elliot leaves, Mendelssohn waits and sips his wine. He rises a little unsteadily on his feet and goes to the bathroom, returns to linger at his dessert. He pays with credit card, signs his bill, makes his way through the rows of empty tables. Both the waitress and the coat-check girl help him with his coat. The detectives would like to tell them to stop, to do something entirely different, to have Mendelssohn sit down, please wait, don't move, stop the world on its curve, decide against whatever it is he is doing, change the course of the world with lethargy.

One click, and then he is gone. What frustrates them most is the outdoor camera, by the front-door foyer. The angle is perfect, but all they can see is Mendelssohn as he steps out into the storm, tugging his collar sharply, tapping his walking stick on the ground, pausing a moment, not visibly upset, moving forward. Thirty-seven seconds later he falls back into the frame, his Homburg spinning from his head. He smashes back against the ground. They see the assailant step into the frame for a fraction of a second. A dark figure bending down as if to whisper something to Mendelssohn. Baseball hat, a puffy jacket. It's always so much easier to solve a case in the summertime—no hats, no scarves, no covered faces. But it's winter and he's a man of indeterminate race, impossible to tell, even in zoom, shadowed and hurried. He appears to have a scarf around his mouth and he wears a hat with curved letters, possibly a *B* or an *8* and a *C* or an *O*. They enhance it further, crop it, copy it, send it to video forensics. At a quarter of a second of digital footage—thirty frames per second—they have 7.5 images of the hat. After four hours of examination, they come back to say that it's *B.C.* braided on the brim. The detectives immediately go to Google to see if Elliot went to Boston College, but Elliot is a Harvard boy through and through. Still, the assailant is someone with enough gumption to wear a Boston hat in Yankeetown.

They split the screen and sift the images as thoroughly as possible, watching only the crucial moments in real time. The rest is speeded up so that there is a silent-movie quality to the footage, Mendelssohn eating quickly, donning his coat, moving herky-jerky toward the door on his walking stick, but then they slow him down as he steps outside, is gone from the image, and then reappears, frozen in midfall, frozen again a second later, his face a gasp of surprise: *How dare you punch me,* before his head cracks open in a pool of dark blood.

There is no camera on the employee entrance, located ten yards down Madison Avenue, a simple metal door that leads past the bathrooms back into the kitchen. The only other obvious angle to the assault is from the traffic-cam on the light pole at Eighty-sixth and Madison: a wide view remotely accessed from traffic control. The quality is low, but the scope is wide. On any other day it might complement the restaurant footage—the tideline of taxis, the baleful swarm of dented trucks—but today it is obscured by snow blowing directly onto the lens, beginning with droplets that melt on the screen at first but then accumulate one by one, coalescing, a gathering curtain of white. It starts with flakes that melt and burn against the heat of the lens, stay a moment, rivulet along the screen. Then they arrive in more rapid flurries. They build, layer, vault upward into the camera, like a crowd of rioters obscuring the crime. At the time of the murder the only thing that can be seen through the granules of snow are the headlights of the approaching cars, small and spectral as they make their way up the avenue. No figures. No faces. No men in baseball caps. No images of an assailant running down the street.

Moments after the assault, the granules pick up the vague swirl of blue-and-red siren lights until eventually the street is closed off and the footage becomes a static portrait of headlights. There is no soundtrack, but the detectives can almost hear the car horns blaring in frustration, until the word *murder* begins to filter among the stalled cars and they fall silent.

The detectives look for cameras in the nearby stores and banks, but there are none with a suitable angle onto the front of Chialli's. Yet they know that there is a solution embedded in the footage somewhere, or perhaps there is another camera to be found in the shops along Madison Avenue, or some other digital eye that is witness to the day. It's a simple logic—a crime has been committed and therefore an answer must be available, somewhere, somehow. Nothing is elementally unsolvable. It's an obvious physical law. If it happened, it can be unraveled. The difficulty comes in the sheer amount of work that must be done to sift through the footage. Even if they find a glimpse of a man in a B.C. hat—in the subway at Lexington Avenue, or walking quickly uptown away from the scene—they will have nothing to tie him directly to the punch.

Just as a poem turns its reader into accomplice, so, too, the detectives become accomplice to the murder. But unlike our poetry, we like our murders to be fully solved: if, of course, it is a murder, or poetry, at all.

VIII

I know noble accents
And lucid, inescapable rhythms;
But I know, too,
That the blackbird is involved
In what I know.

In he walks, a ball of bristle and fear. The phone shoved against his ear. In trouble again, no doubt. He shakes off his overcoat at the coat check. Drips of snowmelt on the floor in a wide constellation. The coat-check girl gives him the once-over. He removes his scarf to reveal a neck that could fold over itself several times. There is something of the ancient walrus about Elliot, imposing and lumbering at the same time. He exposes the big bald head with a whip-off of the hat and gestures across the restaurant with a single finger raised: *Wait for me, but don't expect me to hurry.* He turns away from the coat-check girl and cups his hand over the phone. A serious call indeed. An anger in the bend of his body.

A touch of the Irish about him. Red and veiny. What happened to Eileen's fine genes? Maybe they all went in Katya's direction. Strange how it happens. We never really become fathers to the whole experience. We become, instead, the sons of our sons. What happens to them, then, happens to us. So be it. That's my boy in the corner of the restaurant, shouting now into his cell phone, and here I sit, with a glass of water, watching, and the truth of the matter is that I couldn't love him any more or dislike him any less—the curse of the father. Could somebody please quietly shut him up and guide him over here to my favorite table so that he can shake my hand, maybe even kiss my freckled forehead, say hello, and slide silently into his seat and be the charmer that he once was? Maybe the snow will interrupt the cell-phone signal and we can sit in peace, and when was the last time we actually spoke to each other, not just pleasantries? When oh when did I say a word to him that truly meant something?

He reaches for his glass of water—and thank the heavens, he can see Elliot getting off the telephone. Hurry on now, son, you're making quite a fuss, another fifteen minutes of my life gone to waste.

Snow really hammering down outside now. A swell of intent, slantwise along the street. Mach shnell, son. Join me.

Across the room, Elliot raises his finger once again, this one in apology, or what seems like apology at least, and begins to dial once more.

Oh, to hell with manners, which waitress is mine? Can't remember, though she's been at the table at least twice already. Is it the tall blonde or the small blonde or the medium blonde or the medium-medium blonde with the ponytail? The new manager, it seems, has a stake in a hair-dye company.

He turns in his chair and flicks a look across the room and, sure enough, here she comes the medium-medium blonde with a smile on her face. They grow more beautiful by the year. Either genetics or it's the optics of old age.

—Yes, Mr. Mendelssohn?

—I'd like a glass of Sancerre, my dear.

—Of course, sir.

—And a Cabernet too. For the full-bodied fellow over there.

—Excuse me?

—My son.

—Oh, of course, sir.

She smiles mischievously and swishes her way towards the bar. Oh, for crying out loud, Elliot, get off the phone and stop embarrassing me, please. The temptation of the Apple, the glory of Eve, the confusion of Adam, and what is it with me and the Garden of Eden today? Let me remain with my BlackBerry, dangling on the vine, and did they have any blackberries in Eden, I wonder, to complement the apple trees, and where is it, by the way, the phone? He pats his pockets but it is not there. Must have left it in my coat. Turned up to high volume if I recall correctly. Or was it only on vibrate? That would be embarrassing if the thing starts to ring from afar. No more than six customers in the restaurant today, but that would make the noise even more acute. Please don't let it ring, please. Turn up the music, Dandinho, please. Funny that. It's Mendelssohn. Symphony no. 4. Filtering over the speakers. A nice clean, cool sound, though he can still hear his roiled-up son barking into the telephone. Once upon a time he was a charmer with a garrulous gift, but somewhere along the way it dissolved. Take it outside into the snow, Elliot. If your mother were here, she'd march straight across and give you what-for. And what is it we give our children anyway, except the ability to not become us? How awful the world would be if we were all carbon copies of one another. But Elliot most certainly is not his mother, and maybe I have to face it: he is more me, more's the pity, for him, and for me, and perhaps for the rest of us too.

Here she comes, tray in hand. Sweating nicely: the glass, not the waitress. And a generous pour too: the drink and waitress both.

—You're looking splendid today, young lady.

A speck of blue paint on the inside of her wrist. Probably an artist, they all have second jobs. Abstract, no doubt. A Brooklyn landscape, neat and precise but with a nice rounded swirl.

—Thank you, Mr. Mendelssohn. You're quite dapper yourself.

Oh, how quickly the dark clouds disappear. From diaper to dapper. And she even knows my name. Genuine, it seems: she's not just blowing smoke, like half the waitstaff seem to do every day, their mundanities, nice to see you, have a good day, are you still working on that, sir? I'm *eating*, young lady, not *working*. This medium-medium blonde has style and taste and charisma.

Not just another throwaway. He must remember that come tip-time. He does indeed look—what's the word?—oh, it's fallen off the cliff face, gone, the old Yiddish phrase, there's a few still in the vault, they bob up like Halloween apples, here and there, but what is it? Gone. Still and all, he looks dapper, yes. A Brooks Brothers shirt. A Gucci tie selected by Sally. A beautifully cut suit made for him by none other than Frankie Shattuck, the young boxer-tailor-soldier-sailor. The best damn suitmaker in New York. Good creases in the trousers. A beautifully finished collar. Silk lining. The clothes indeed make the man. When he was appointed to the Circuit Court, decades ago, he went straight down to the tailorshop to ask Frankie's father to make him a proper judicial gown and that he did, the finest cloth, the most perfect stitches, the proper pockets, the right hang from his shoulders, the space inside to greet and gavel, *farpitz*—that's the word, yes, *farpitz*. And he got one with an even finer cut of cloth when he got elected to the Supreme Court. Gone now, Frankie's father. All of us fading like the morning dew. Our Yiddish too.

—Terrible weather, says the waitress.

—When I was a boy it snowed ten times worse.

Which is not true at all. He can only remember Vilnius in the summertime.

—I never saw a snowflake until I moved here, she says.

—Australia?

—No.

—New Zealand?

—No.

She's toying with me now: South Africa?

—Zimbabwe, she says, with a flourish.

Oh, toy and tarry. What a city this is. Never ceases to amaze me. A blonde Rhodesian girl serving a Polish-born Lithuanian Jew in an Italian restaurant with, what, a couple of Mexican busboys hanging out near the edges, ready to pounce, and of course Dandinho, the Brazilian busboy extraordinaire moving gracefully from table to table, and my big bald American son yammering away on the telephone by the coat check.

—And your name is?

—Rosita.

—Why, thank you, Rosita.

An unusual name for a girl from Africa. She smiles as she backs away. He nods at Dandinho who moves swiftly across to fill up his water glass.

—Thirsty today, sir?

—It's the heat outside, young man.

Dandinho pours with great panache, one hand kept behind his back, as if his whole body is paying respect to the water glass. Not afraid to get his hands wet. An all-rounder. A meeter, a greeter, a half maître d'. Known far and wide for the way he can wrap your leftovers. An aluminum artist. No mean skill that. Nothing to snigger at. A folder of the foil. He can create any shape the diner wants—swan or porpoise or cow or crane or giraffe. Within seconds the leftovers become a work of art. A doggie bag, indeed. The kids love it but so do the ladies who lunch and indeed so do the late-night businessmen going home with an exotic aluminum animal under the arm. There was even, a few years ago, a gallery downtown that put on an exhibition of Dandinho's foil sculptures.

—How're you feeling today, sir?

—A million bucks. All torn and wrinkly.

A tolerant smile from Dandinho: he's heard the quip before.

—Anything else, Mr. Mendelssohn?

—Fine for now. Waiting in fact for my son.

—Ah, yes. Some bread?

—Thank you, Dandinho, but I'm watching my figure.

And here he comes at last, lumbering across, hardly a figure skater, bumping off the tables and chairs. Tucking away his phone as he goes. Still there is an energy about him, nothing small or meek, that's for sure, three Mendelssohns in one movement, father, son, symphony.

—Dad, he says, with a kind swerve in his voice, and a grasp of his father's shoulder.

A bit of weight on him, sure, but he still has a pair of fine, bright eyes, the same shape as his mother's. Speak to me of her, son, in a pattering hail-shower of words.

—Elliot, meet Dandinho.

—A pleasure, sir.

—My pleasure, Davido.

Elliot grasps Dandinho's hand and doles out a big handshake. He'd make a good politician, even if he keeps getting names wrong. A sharp dresser too. Gold tiepin. Straight collar. Fine-cut cloth.

—Elliot Mendelssohn, he says, Barner Funds.

As if Dandinho gives a flying fig about Barner Funds, but the Brazilian pauses a moment, then reaches behind Elliot's chair and holds it politely, scoots it in, or hardly scoots it at all, given Elliot's proportions. Elliot shifts on the chair like it's a dangerous horse. The table shivers a little and the silverware clangs.

—Thank you, Davido.

An odd look on Dandinho's face, something rattling through his mind, a bronco, a bull, a bear. Is it possible that Dandinho speculates? One never knows. The unlikeliest of people get themselves into the market these days and who knows what sort of life goes on behind another life? Maybe Dandinho has himself a fine big mansion out there in Brooklyn somewhere, goldplated handles, swimming pool, a Jacintha wife, the whole nine yards, the NASDAQ pulsing in neon around his shaving mirror, stranger things have happened, even to an aging busboy.

—A very solid firm, sir.

—You invest there, Dandinho?

—Oh, no, sir, not me, Mr. Mendelssohn. I just know some people.

—Don't we all? says Elliot.

Dandinho nods and backs away.

The menu-flip. The napkin unfold. The usual pleasantries. Great to see you, son. Terrible weather. Sorry I'm late. A drone of excuses, more sound than meaning—he got caught in work, was waylaid on Lexington, some business deal fouled up along the way, he's just swamped these days, time, time, time.

A fine wine of a man to make excuses: he gets better with age.

—I took the liberty.

—Thanks, Dad.

—A Cabernet for you, sir.

Elliot pretends not to take an eyeful as Rosita leans across him and places the wine down. She stands with her hands on the low of her stomach as she enumerates the specials. Quite a pose. That little speck of blue on her wrist: such a perfect addition, like the wrongly tied knot on a Persian carpet.

—Thank you, Rosita.

Salmon with dill sauce for him. A porterhouse steak, medium rare, with mango sauce for Elliot. No appetizers. Straight to the heart of the matter. She scribbles it down on a small blue pad, bats her eyelids, moves away, yes, an artist, no doubt. Salmon indeed. Watch her sway upriver, a fine expanse of flank.

—L'chaim, says Elliot.

So often the boy for the opportune word, there has recently been talk of Elliot running for office, a disastrous move, no doubt, even for a *macher* like him—they would chew him up and spit him out and freeze-dry him in the process—but who's to fault ambition? And here we go, clinking glasses and diving into the old murky water, father and son, and how is Jacintha, and what's happening at home, any news from Katya, all smooth with Sally, do you ever use the motorized chair, are you eating well enough, have you seen Dr. Marion?

They are halfway through their wine when Elliot's phone rings.

—Excuse me.

A woman's voice from the sound of things. Elliot is quick and curt. Yes, no, I can't talk right now, absolutely not, she doesn't have a case, forget it, I said I can't talk right now.

He shuts the phone and says: Jesus H.

And why in the world is the *H* always thrown in there? *Our Father, who art in Heaven, Harold be thy name.* Eileen once said: Why not *A* for *Art*? *Our Father, who is Art in Heaven.* Or sling them both together? *Jesus H. A. Christ.*

Elliot presses the phone down on the table, fingers some buttons, a piano player, even with his big meaty hands, a Richter of the keyboard.

—You're a busy man, Elliot.

—Just work stuff, sorry. It never stops.

—Lady problems?

—Aren't they all?

He deserves a good clip on the ear for that one. Good thing Eileen's not around, she'd whip him silly, march him into the bathroom and soap his mouth out.

—My secretary.

—I see.

—Had to fire her.

—Sorry to hear that.

—She's trying to sue me.

—That's not good.

—Give them an inch, they take a mile. Bitcharita.

A sting of a word. A shot of Patrón. Salt on the wound.

Bitcharita. An immigrant to the language. Beyond the blonde
wives, Elliot always had a bit of an eye for the Latin girls.

—Sounds complicated.

Elliot flicks a look off into the distance. A little tremble of his
eyelid and a twist of the mouth. Impossible to forget that he was
once six years old, out on the beach in Long Island, blue shorts,
a patch of dry sand on his shoulder, leaning against his mother's
shoulder, a sandwich in his hand, Eileen's arm around his waist,
the waves rolling up to shore, when he was the boy he seemed
destined to be.

And there it is again, shimmying and shaking, vibrating on
the table, what is this, *Candid Camera?*

—Sorry, Dad.

—Oh, that's okay, go ahead, take it, really, it's okay.

Though it's not okay, it's far from okay, it's light years from
okay—just do the right thing and turn the phone off, would
you, please, son, keep Allen Funt locked in the kitchen, smile,
you're the star of the show, oh, the mind is a trampoline today, it
was Allen Funt, wasn't it? They were good years, uncompli-
cated, or so they seemed anyway, we gathered around the television together for the nightly shows, a long thin Elliot sprawled
out on the carpet, Katya curled into her beanbag, he and Eileen
in matching armchairs, the room was cozy, the fire was lit, there
were belted ashtrays that hung around the arm of the chairs, and
he smoked a pipe then, I haven't touched a pipe in I don't know
how long, haven't even smelled a cigarette for years.

A strong insistent whisper this time: I told you, I'm having lunch, don't call me with this bullshit again.

Then a dip towards his wineglass: Sorry, Dad.

—Do you remember when they used to allow you to smoke in restaurants?

—Excuse me?

—I was just thinking about how everyone used to smoke. I still have the pipe, you know. In the bedroom.

—Nobody smokes pipes anymore, Dad.

—You can still smell the smoke in the bowl. If you put it to your nose. It lingers.

Elliot glances down at the phone again. And what is it that lingers anymore? Really what I want to talk to you about is those old days with your mother, when we were all together, and life rolled along, slow enough, day to day, and why is it that we complicate the past, is it simply just pipesmoke? But here we are, listening to you prattle about the *bitcharita* and yet another excuse for being late, and surely there's something else, son? Should I have another try at my memoirs? Should I give Sally James a raise? Would you like another glass of Cabernet? How in the world are you going to fill that five-car garage? Could a man even poison himself with carbon monoxide in a place that big? No, no, tell me this and tell me no more: Do you miss your mother, son? Or tell me this: Do you recall the days we spent at the beach in Oyster Bay? Or tell me this: Do you ever return to the thought of her with the hint of a sigh?

And there it is again, the goddamn phone bronco-bucking on the table. From across the room come a few darting looks. He's not mine, I promise you, he's an alien—they make them big and blue-eyed and American now. A tut-tut from one of the Ladies Who Lunch, and a sympathetic tilt of the head from the waitress.

Rosita, Maid Marion, come rescue me, cart my son out into the snow, deposit him there, bring your bow and arrow, take careful aim, and shoot the fucking Apple off his head like Robin Hood, or indeed William Burroughs.

Elliot leans across and with the charm of which he is sometimes capable says: Do you mind, Father? I really have to take this one.

Do I what? Of course I mind. Here we are, breaking bread, and all you want to do is jabber on endlessly. There was once a time when you'd sit in the kitchen alcove, and we'd lean together over mathematics, quadrangles, quadratics, as close as any two could get, multiplied by one another. How long has it been since we actually looked at each other, tell me that, son. I'm a sentimental old fool, I'm dripping with nostalgia, but cynics bore me, and I might as well wear my heart on my sleeve, I'd like to talk to you without interruption, can you give me at least that?

—No problem, Elliot.

—Thanks, Dad.

He turns sideways in the chair, cups his hand over the phone, his big gold wedding ring shining. Hear no evil, see no evil, speak no evil. A silver bracelet on his wrist. To keep the vampires away. Didn't work with Jacintha, that's for sure. There is something afoot with Elliot, he can hear bits and pieces coming in his direction, a male voice this time, he jigsaws them both together, she was fired, fair and square, that's extortion, there's just no way, I'll sue her, how dare she, who does she think she is, she's a goddamn secretary, I don't give a fuck what she calls it, look, Dave, I'm in a restaurant with my father, she just can't, can you give me an hour, it was fair and square—goddammit, just take care of it, would you?—that's what I pay you for, she wants a lawsuit she'll get a lawsuit, executive assistant my ass, bring it on.

More to it always than meets the eye. How many women have slung accusations Elliot's way? *Hi, Barner Funds, Elliot Mendelssohn's office, how can I help you?* Save me a place in the unemployment line please, my boss just called me a bitcharita.

—Sorry, Dad, he says again, rolling his eyes at the phone and leaning across the table to take some bread from the basket.

No worries, son, I'll just sit here awaiting my salmon with dill sauce and let the lazy day drift away.

—I'll be right with you, I promise.

And there he goes with the finger again, and a shake of his jowls—he looks farm-caught himself, open-mouthed—and he is scooting back his chair, half the restaurant looking at him, hook, line, sinker.

Where in the world did I go wrong, did I ruin his childhood, did I neglect him, did I not read the right books to him, did I drop him on the crown of his early bald head? He came through the teenage years with flying colors, never caused too many problems. A good-looking kid, came home with his lacrosse trophies, debate certificates, chess medals. No late-night phone calls. No suspensions. No arrests. Amherst, then Harvard, got himself to Wall Street, hunkered down for a couple of years, played the money game, rolled the ball, made it round, but just look at him now, walking past the empty tables, towards the restrooms, watched by Dandinho all the way. An odd look on Dandinho's face. Surely he's seen many a customer chatting on the phone, cheating on the phone even? Maybe there's a house rule against it, cheating and chatting?

I could do with another glass of Sancerre, where's my medium-medium blonde, come to me, what is your name again, Rosita, Rosita, my stem, my petal, my thorn.

IX

When the blackbird flew out of sight,
It marked the edge
Of one of many circles.

If only real life could have the logic of the written word: characters with conscious actions, hidden causes becoming plain, all things moving toward a singular point, the universe revealing itself as inexorably stable, everything boiled down to a static image, controlled, ordered, logical. In a simple world it should have been a straightforward Jewish funeral, but Mendelssohn was an atheist, or so it was said anyway, agnostic at least, though he certainly had a touch of tradition to him, and he wasn't averse to playing whatever card suited him. He had married a Catholic woman, and the children were raised between religions, and Mendelssohn himself had confessed to being Jewish when he wanted to be, and Lithuanian most of the time, but Polish if he needed to be, a touch of Russian if so charged, an American in most respects, an occasional European, even Irish every once in a while by virtue of his wife. A mongrel really, a true New Yorker, in a city where people never knew how to die. Cremation. Exhalation. Annihilation. A proper Jewish ceremony would have seen him buried as soon as possible, but then there was the issue of an autopsy and the delay of Mendelssohn's daughter all the way from Tel Aviv, and the political aspirations of the son, and where his wife, Eileen, was buried, and whether his ashes should be scattered or not, and what he might have written in his will, and who might have had access to his very last wishes.

The service takes place on Amsterdam Avenue in the late morning, five days after the assault. The snow has turned to slush and there are deep puddles by the curbsides where the cars pull in. A sad splash of wheels in the potholes. It is a high, wide angle, but a good grade of footage: every funeral home in the city has its own series of hidden surveillance cameras. The detectives have, over the years, become watchers of funerals. It often surprises them that there are not more services on reality TV: there is something so compulsively informative about them. The way life gets played out in death. The manner in which the widow falls to her knees. Or not. The way in which the son shoulders the weight of the coffin. Or not. The way the father becomes the sole proprietor of the daughter's death. Or not. The enigmatic notes arriving with the flowers. Or not. The subtle dig put in the eulogy by the rabbi, the priest, the imam, the vicar, the monk. Funerals as indicators of a life, how it was lived, the amount of tears shed, the keening and the rending of clothes, the sheer volume of mourners who choose to show up, the length of time people hang around afterward, the very nature of the way they hold their bodies. It has even struck them at times that they can tell some of the sexual predilections of the deceased just by looking at the clothes the mourners wear: the higher the hemline, the more ambitious the life. Hardly a mathematical formula, but then again so many things are unexplainable, and how is it that we know a life, except that we know our own, and it is brought into focus by the death of those around us.

Elliot is the first of the family to arrive. He steps out from his dark limousine and, interestingly enough, does not go to the other side of the car to help his wife emerge. Rather, he stands in the middle of the pavement and gazes up at the name of the funeral home as if he wants to read some deep significance into it. No outward sign of sorrow, though he still wears a torn black ribbon over his heart, a gesture at least to ancient tradition. His wife is a pile-up of peroxide. She stands alongside him, both together and apart. She has three children from previous marriages, and they step out from the car as if part of a moon landing, teenage boys, all gangle and long hair, looking as if they are already bored with their own patented slouch.

Elliot nods at them, checks his watch, consults his cell phone, a man distracted.

The daughter arrives ten minutes after Elliot. Katya Atkinson. Dark-eyed with grief and travel. She looks younger: early fifties maybe. She wears a dark skirt and a matching jacket.

There is something fierce and intelligent about her. A streak of gray in her hair. She steps her agile way over the curbside puddle, toward her brother. Elliot leans down to give her a perfunctory kiss on the cheek.

Together, brother and sister step toward the funeral home and are soon engulfed by others who have arrived almost simultaneously in a polite wave: judges, office workers, neighbors. The super and the doormen, including Tony DiSalvo. Sally James. At least one hundred people. Among them, too, the restaurant manager, Christopher Eagleton, and the busboy, Dandinho, who, upon his appearance, is marked as a person of significant suspicion: why in the world would the busboy arrive at the funeral?

The detectives return again to the restaurant footage, but Dandinho never leaves the building, not once, he simply has his animated conversation with Pedro Jiménez by the dishwashing station, and he is most certainly located on the footage by the bar when the punch is thrown outside the restaurant. Dandinho is, in fact, one of the first to go to Mendelssohn's aid when he falls. He is calm and controlled when questioned, not a hint of guilt about him, keen to point out that Mendelssohn was one of his favorite customers, that he always took home his leftovers for his housekeeper, tipped well, was old-world, polite, a hint of a twinkle still in his eye. He did not witness the actual punch, although he heard the thump of the old man's head on the pavement, he thought at first that maybe Mendelssohn had just slipped on the ice, but he knew immediately that he was dead, an awful thing, he felt very sorry for him, a terrible way to go, he went to the funeral to pay his respects, it was the Christian thing to do.

Although still a person of interest, the detectives rule Dandinho out. Same, too, with Eagleton.

They comb the funeral footage, looking for any other face or body language that might strike them as needing attention—they push in, push out, brush forward, rewind, bookmark what they find interesting, but there is nothing more compelling than the appearance of the middle-aged busboy.

And so, like the snow, or the latter point in a poem, the theories drift across the screen, opposition and conflict, so many possibilities available to the detectives, all of them intersecting in various ways, a Venn diagram of intent, the real world presenting itself with all its mystery—is it a murder of inheritance, a murder of jealousy, a murder of retribution, a murder of bitterness, or a murder simply tied to the random? They cannot discount the notion that it could be tied to an old case of Mendelssohn's, a resurfacing on an anniversary, or a con just out of prison after serving a long sentence, or a specific grudge that has been left many years in abeyance, even though Mendelssohn has been retired from Kings County for six years and the detectives are unable to pinpoint any obvious cases likely to have left him with such a long-term enemy. A few gangland murders. The Screaming Phantoms, the Driggs Boys of Justice, the Tikwando Brothers, the Dirty Ones, the Vanguards, the Black Hands. Several minor Mafia figures and an early encoun-

ter with Roy DeMeo but no conviction. Some corruption cases.
Break-ins. Carjackings. A high-profile city discrimination case
in the late 1980s. Thousands of minor cases over the years. He
was well liked in the corridors of Adams Street. He was known
to spar verbally with the lawyers, but had a reputation as a rela-
tively soft judge, a man of light sentence. No significant anni-
versaries. No candidates recently released from prison. Who
would wait over a decade to extract revenge? Could it be that
Sally James gave someone the nod along Madison Avenue and
pointed him out? After all, Elliot Mendelssohn had installed
cameras in the apartment to watch her, and he was aware that
Sally had been given a generous stipend in the will to look after
her nephew's education. Or could it be that Elliot himself
wanted to hurry up the inheritance? Perhaps he has some financial problems? When they question him about his restaurant
phone calls he admits to having had a dalliance with his secretary, Maria Casillas, having recently fired her. Perhaps he was
upset at something his father said to him? It is not beyond possibility that the anger built up inside him and he snapped. Or
that he hired someone to snap on his behalf. Or perhaps there
could be a tie-in with Katya, someone keen to wreck the final
tatters of the Mideast peace process? But why would they do
that in New York rather than Israel, and why would they go
after her father rather than her? Could it be something that
Mendelssohn said on his way out of the restaurant, just a glancing comment that elicited anger from a passerby? But there
have been no other incidents along the street, on Park or Fifth

or even down Lexington, and when they check the subway cameras they cannot locate anyone at all in a puffy jacket or a Boston College hat: it is as if the attacker has disappeared into thin air.

They play it again in their minds, in light of everything they already know. It is their hope that each moment, when ground down and sifted through, examined and prodded, read and re-read, will yield a little more of the killer and the world he, or she, has created. They go forward metrically, and then break time again. They return, judge, reconfigure. They weigh it up and take stock, sift through, over and over. The breakthrough is there somewhere in the rhythmic disjunctions, in the small re-suscitations of language, in the fractured framework.

The closest they have come to the killer is still in the footage just outside the restaurant where he steps into the frame for a quarter second in his jacket and hat, a man, most likely, bending over the body of Mendelssohn, maybe to check if he is alive, maybe to whisper some obscenity. The attacker pulls back and out of the frame and there is nothing more they can tell about him. He is, in essence, just a hat and a shadow. Moments later it is Dandinho bending over the old man, then the restaurant manager, Eagleton, followed by the waitress and the coat-check girl, and within minutes Mendelssohn is surrounded by dozens of passersby, the blood rivering from him, his hat fallen sideways, the bag of leftovers on the ground, a leak of dill sauce into the snow.

They rewind and freeze the attacker in his B.C. hat. Strange that, to come all the way from Boston. Or at least to showcase it in a rival city. And it is then that it hits them—one of those odd moments, when the truth comes in a sharp little slice, opening the echo chambers, releasing the synapses—that they may have been thinking in the wrong direction for quite a while now, and they have been flummoxed by their own preconceptions, like archaeologists, or critics, or literary scholars, and that it is so much more simple than they want it to be, and much of it lies in the attacker's hat, the most available piece of evidence, but perhaps it is not a Boston College hat at all, but it could have any number of meanings, British Columbia, or a rock band, or the comic strip, an endless litany of *B.C.*'s, maybe even personal initials, but it could also possibly be the Brooklyn Cyclones, a minor-league team, yes, but a staple of the New York imagination, and this is the moment when the smallest of things becomes the linchpin, when the pit in the stomach grows, so that when the detectives google the Brooklyn Cyclones, they realize that the hats do have a similar texture to Boston College, the *C* braided into the *B,* they could easily be mistaken for one another, almost identical, especially in the off-color of the video images, the only difference being that the Boston College hat nearly always has an eagle braided into the brim, and how come they overlooked such a simple notion is beyond them, yes, of course, it must be the Cyclones, given that it's closer to home, and perhaps then the killer is from Brooklyn, and wasn't there somewhere along the course of the investigation that they saw a Brooklyn Cyclones reference, someone wearing a T-shirt, or something along those lines, a poster perhaps, yes, a poster, didn't it creep along their sightlines, didn't they make a vague note of it earlier when they were casting around? Or is it one of the recipients of Mendelssohn's justice in Brooklyn long ago, a grudge revisited, did the Cyclones somehow creep into his litany of cases? Or is it just their imaginations and have the Cyclones never been mentioned at all?

In the hands of the detectives, the past never stops happening. They dive backward, with their spiral notepads, into the early verses of their work.

X

At the sight of blackbirds
Flying in a green light,
Even the bawds of euphony
Would cry out sharply.

One is too little, two is never enough. Another glass of Sancerre, please, my dear, then cut me off. Alexander the Great knew when and where to stop. It used to be, long ago long ago, that he could put away five, six glasses, but those days are gone, and his army has long since retreated.

In his early years there was the curious practice of the three-martini lunch. The Queen on Court Street. Luger's on Broadway. Marco Polo's in Carroll Gardens. But it was Gage and Tollner on Fulton Street that was the best of them all. Sunlight through the window. Motes of dust in the slanted shaftways. The gimlet hour. A spot of lime and soda, please. How in the world did the system operate when so much of the world was liquored up and tongue-loosened? You never quite knew what way the afternoon would swing. But he saw some great performances in his courtroom back in the day, lawyers who could spin out the most elegant of phrases when gin-lit. Standing up in the courtroom in slightly rumpled suits and ties, slurring, too, but still able to sling the sentences against sentence. Dan Barry, the best of them all. And Dwyer. And Cohen. And Dowd. All lawyer's lawyers. They were sharpest in the morning. Their arguments could cut through steel. Come noon the world would grow fidgety. It was said that the worst time to finish a case was late in the afternoon when the judges were irritable and ready to go home. It was even worse earlier in the week, when they weren't yet draped in the promise of a weekend's respite. But for him, the energy would pick up with the assurance of escape from the gun barrels, the knifeblades, the razors, the meat cleavers, the endless parade of nightsticks and broken bottles. All that misery. It was as if, all of a sudden, the day had church bells in it, ringing again around four thirty as he sat in chambers, poring over evidence, or writing a judgment, or signing off on the endless paperwork which was, in itself, another form of mindless violence. Wake up, wake up, your day's almost done. No more rapists. No more conmen. No more arsonists. No more shoplifters. No more stalkers. No more illiterate cops. It was like his own little get-out-of-jail-free card. The sun was going down, but the light was coming up. He never hung around for the evenings' tomfoolery when the rest of them disappeared into the watering holes of Brooklyn, P. J. Hanley's, the Inn, Buzzy's place down by the waterfront. He caught a bit of shrapnel from within the party apparatus for moving to the Upper East Side, but he didn't mind so much, it wasn't incumbent on him to live in Brooklyn. He was off home to Eileen, driving across the bridge, no subway for him. The reverse commute. A lovely thing to see the sun fully disappear, a fine red aspirin swallowed by the city. He parked the car in the garage off Park Avenue. She would be waiting for him, in the kitchen, in her apron, dusting off her hands before she kissed him. He poured a stiff Scotch and headed straight for the deep leather armchair. How odd to live two such separate lives. He dozed off in the chair and woke to Eileen boiling up a cup of warm milk, his nightly mugshot.

Every now and then, Thanksgiving, Passover, Christmas, he'd stay out with the bigwigs in Brooklyn for a late night, or they'd drift their way to Manhattan, to the Lion's Head, or McSorley's, many of them Irish and paying the price for it. They thought of him as their Hibernian Jew: his accent still had a faint hint of the Dublin days and of course there was Eileen, reading aloud to him, putting what she called the *rozziner* in his language. The Irish war songs were merry, their love songs sad. They'd be there, in the courtrooms, the very next morning, after breakfast in Teresa's on Montague, a little red around the eyelids, Janus-faced, but fully operational all the same. Keenan, Rhodes, Potter, McDonald, Jewell. Characters, all and sundry. Destined for heaven or hell, they didn't really care that much. They were out and about, extracting life from life. What matter if half their clientele ended up on probation, or even worse, in jail? They had done their jobs. They had argued well. It was whiskey now, the water of life. Pour or be poured.

And how is it that the deep past is littered with the characters, while the present is so housebroken and flat? Wasn't it Faulkner who said that the past is not dead, it's not even past? Funny thing, the present tense. Technically it cannot exist at all. Once we're aware of it, it's gone, no longer present. We dwell, then, in the constant past, even when we're dreaming of the future. Surely that's a theme of some Shakespearean sonnet or other, though I can hardly remember them, waves coming towards the shore, our hastening minutes, our secret toil.

Oh, the head is spinning. Too much wine. The grapes of wrath. One is too little, and two is never enough. Words, it seems, that young Elliot has taken to heart, out there in the bathroom, or the restroom, or the john, or the jacks, or the *vanetsimer,* or the *pishen* hole, or whatever they call it nowadays. Gone ten, fifteen minutes. Take a good look in *der shpigl,* young man, and tell me what it is you see. He always was a boy vain for the mirror, especially in his college days, glancing at himself sideways every chance he got, that long blond hair on him.

How quickly the bright child becomes the ruined man. One is too little, two is often enough.

It was always Katya to whom he gravitated anyway. Quite the girl. A handful in her early years. An Upper East Side Marxist. At thirteen she sheared her hair. Then, a year later, got herself a nose ring. Wore a Che Guevara T-shirt on the few occasions that they went to temple together. She forged his signature on several checks that were made out to the Black Panthers. It started out in twenty-dollar installments, but ended up with one thousand. He learned about it through an article in the *New York Post*. He was not amused. He was the butt of jokes left, right, and center. They took, in the judicial corridors, to calling him Malcolm X. For her sixteenth birthday she sent her own check for five hundred dollars, but by then the novelty had worn off and she took, instead, to dropping the family's china out the rear window of the apartment. Out with the footed cups and saucer plates! Out with the coupe soup bowls! Out with the tiered serving tray! Out with the immaculate gravy boat! *¡Viva la revolución!* Who needs butter plates anyway? Let's see how the sterling silver bounces! Hark, the serving platters sing! The courtyard was like an echo chamber. She loved how finely it splintered: apparently the sign of good china was how minutely it broke. They lived on the sixth floor, so there was time enough to hear the Waterford whistle. Several of the downstairs neighbors opened their windows and shouted at her to stop, but secretly they were surely interested in the sailing symphony. Stop, please stop, Katya, stop. Okay, if you must, just one more demitasse, please, my dear.

She went through a few thousand dollars' worth of china over the course of two nights. The best punishment was no punishment at all. He went and kissed her sleeping forehead. A judge didn't judge, not his own daughter anyway. She was into her military industrial complex by then. Ranted and raved and roared. Said he was having an obvious love affair with Nixon.

Made Calvin Coolidge look like a liberal. Was interested to know if he'd like to buy body bags for all the students in her classroom. A government garment, she said. No pockets in a shroud. Went out in the streets with a loudspeaker, all five foot two of her, screaming through the canyonlands. Occidental death, she called it. But they all turn around in the end, anyway. Or some of them do anyway. She went out west to Berkeley where they put some manners on her, much to his surprise. Oriental Studies. Did her thesis on Ptolemy the Second. The Book of Optics. Vision occurs in the brain rather than the eyes. And isn't that the truth? Went on to the State Department then. Agitating for peace while the rest of them made war. The argument for war has an easy gravity, she told him, but the one for peace does not. A smart cookie, Katya, even if she went out there to Israel, the one place on earth where it was guaranteed not to happen, at least not in this lifetime. You might as well try to turn the wine back into water.

—Would you like me to keep your son's plate warm, Mr. Mendelssohn?

—That's okay, Rosita.

—How's your salmon?

—Oh, it's good, very good.

Though he has hardly tasted a bite, if truth be told. Not a nourishing way to get through the day. Should have just had lunch on my own rather than invite Elliot along. So much better to sit in an accepted silence than have it enforced. That was something that Katya has learned no doubt: the power of silence. Broke her heart not to see peace. Came so close and then got whiskered away. What was his name? Arafat. To which Eileen once whispered: Ara-fat-lot-of-good-he-is-anyway. Always a woman for the fine Gaelic twist. Don't put all your begs in one ask-it.

—Is it ever going to stop snowing?

—Doesn't seem like it, Mr. Mendelssohn.

Oh, the way she rolls her *m*'s, I bet she's great with *p*'s and *q*'s. Should tell her the story of how I became Quinner, though I can't quite even remember it myself. Was it simply the sound of the word? Dublin was a good place. Always reminds me of hats.

We leap from cliff edge to cliff edge. Falling occasionally to the ground, sometimes with a good smack, but that's part of the bargain with age. The memories are still agile enough. Thank God above I never went the Alzheimer's route. Couldn't stand the thought of a nursing home. A dark little room at the end of the corridor, somewhere in Queens or the Bronx or Tobago. The heating on too high. The flowers wilting in a grimy little vase. The nurses with a penchant for a backhand smack. Imagine all life coming down to that. Though they say certain ones among them could be lively enough. All those younger widows still willing and able to disappear beneath the covers. He heard once that the incidence of disease is highest of all in nursing homes. One last hurrah. Any port in a storm. The welts and boils hardly matter at that stage. Odd to think that there could ever be another love affair. Wonder if Sally ever thought of it, alone there in her little room, her small TV set, her playing cards on her little table? Solitaire. The only game in town. Would make for a great Hollywood epic that, the Supreme Court justice and his housekeeping nurse, double duty, finally shacking up after all those years. Conflict, drama, resolution. Roll up, roll under. Get your tickets today. He could sign another portion of the will over to her. Her nephew would get a fine schooling then. Perhaps that's what I should do? Go right home and take out the pages from the files and put that boy further in the will, to hell or high water with Elliot and everyone else. Wouldn't really cost that much. What is it Sally gets a week? Five hundred with room and board? That's twenty-five grand a year, most of which she probably sends back. Could save that boy's life with an extra ten thousand dollars. A drop in the bucket really. A fine lot better than slinging it Elliot's way, although Katya might bear some of the brunt, and those beautiful kids I seldom see. Still and all, she has enough, his Katya, and how in the world did I get here anyway? Alzheimer's. That's the thing. Don't have it now, probably never will. Would forget about it if I did. Isn't that right, Eileen? What an awful thing it would be to forget your own wife, though. Though, there are times when he opens a door, or wakes in the morning, and he's sure she's still there. Good morning, *mo chroí*. What am I doing out here on my own? Jilted by my own son.

Rosita, my dear, I lied to you. The salmon is rubbery. The dill sauce is too milky. I feel like I'm back in the Waldorf Astoria. And really I just want to go home to Eileen. Wrap it up there in two white cloths, Dandinho, let me go.

—Sorry, Dad.

Surprise, surprise. Kill the fatted calf. Elliot parks his large carcass in the seat opposite, his face engine-red. Just short of steam coming out of his ears. Tie a blood-pressure cuff around his arm and the needle might break the glass. He's a certain candidate for a heart attack if he keeps this up. And why in the world would he be fooling around with his assistant anyway? Would he not go the way of that other Elliot, the Spitzer boy, with one *l,* destined for h-e-l—but he was bright enough at least to cough up a few shekels for a bit of companionship?

Elliot pushes his plate forward on the table top.

—Listen, I'm going to have to take care of a few things. . . .

—Okay.

—At the office.

—You haven't even touched your food.

—Just get it wrapped, Dad. Take it home. Give it to— whatshername?

—Sally.

—That's right.

Elliot flicks another look at his phone.

—Is everything okay, El?

He hasn't called him by the diminutive in years. The elevated track. Is everything okay? If that's not the stupidest question I ever asked, I don't know what is. But it doesn't seem to register with Elliot at all, neither the question nor the name. The boy seems distracted beyond language. He turns in the seat and clicks his fingers, then rubs them together like he's divining money. Dandinho stands over in the corner, looking straight ahead. Most certainly something on that man's mind. And what was it about Ptolemy? The truth of sight. He darkened his room and set up a camera obscura on the balcony. The first man to successfully project an entire image from outside onto a screen indoors. That's what Katya said. A ray of light could not proceed from the eyes. Rather, light was the thing that proceeded towards the eye. The outside world giving to the world inside. He's never seen Dandinho be anything but polite, but here he is now, fuming in the corner, a light from his eyes looking like it could scorch a path through the restaurant.

—Tell me this, Elliot.

Clicking his fingers again, over his shoulder, like some Arab prince. No friend of Aristotle's. He feigned madness to keep himself out of prison.

—Did you have words with Dandinho?

—Davido?

—It's Dandinho. He's Brazilian. The busboy.

—Never saw him before in my life.

—He looks a bit upset.

—Wouldn't you be? A busboy at his age?

On a roll now. The anger all sharp-angled. Slapping his credit card down on the table.

—Where's our waitress?

Was Ptolemy happy to know what he knew? Is Katya happy to keep on struggling? Is Sally happy to wake up in the morning? Not much happiness here in Elliot, that's for sure. He has the wife, the car, the garage, the job, the kids, but there's no joy there at all. Used to have it, long ago. A dark magician. Lost it up his sleeve.

—It's on me, Elliot.

His son still clicking his fingers in Dandinho's direction.

—Good place, this, to open a restaurant.

—My treat, I insist.

—Where the hell is she?

—Rosita.

—What?

—Rosita's her name.

—I don't need her name, Dad, I just need the bill. Sorry. I know, I know. I just, I have some stuff I really have to take care of. An hour ago. I called you. I should have—

Ah, the tremble in my pocket on the street. So the ringer is off after all.

—I told you, son, it's my pleasure.

He watches as Dandinho passes along the back of the restaurant, carrying the water jug.

—Jesus, says Elliot.

Without the *H*. Or the *A*. No joy at all.

None and sweet fuck-all.

—Next week, Dad, I promise.

Finally she comes around the corner, her long blond locks bouncing. Thirty-two perfect shining white teeth. A pair of sharp blue eyes. A girl destined for the big screen, surely, but didn't she tell him earlier that she was an artist? Or did he just surmise that? There was a touch of blue on the inside of her wrist, wasn't there?

—Rosita, my dear, this is my bill.

—No way, Dad.

—Look, you haven't even had a bite. Rosita and I have an understanding, isn't that right, Rosita?

Smiling her great big Rhodesian Zimbabwean smile.

—Doesn't the home player get the advantage?

—Sir?

—I mean, I'm the local here, am I not?

A small amount of confusion hovering at the edges of her mouth.

—Besides, he says, I haven't even ordered dessert.

Shifting her weight from foot to foot, she smiles down at Elliot, a thin regal smile.

—I guess your dad wins, she says.

—I guess he does, says Elliot.

And, just like that, he has tucked the credit card away in his shiny brown wallet, as if he had never intended to pay at all. He taps the wallet like the head of a friendly dog. You're not really serious, are you, son? Just like that? Not an ounce of irony? One two three and then away? Like shit off a shovel? Aren't we supposed to at least play a little bit of bob-and-weave? Isn't that what the etiquette demands? You jab, I jab, you duck, I don't. Who raised you anyway? What barn door opened up and tossed you out? Never touched the boy once in my life, but, ay, he deserves a good rap across the wrist now. Bring Katya along and have her produce peace at this table. The last time I fought with anyone was along the Royal Canal when I fell, ten pins down, after a single slap from some carrot-headed Gypsy boy. It rocked a tooth loose in the back of my jaw. The tongue went to it over and over again. A probe of pain. Like fatherhood. Trying to ease those little aches that spring up each and every day. The promise of consolation outlasting the punishment of living.

—So you're off then?

—You know.

No, I don't know, not really.

—Shit happens, Dad.

Indeed, it does. Just ask Sally James.

Oh, the morning seems so distant to me now. *Gay ga*ʒ*inta hate*. That fine doublespeak. Eileen adopted that phrase when she heard it, she loved to say it over and over, at the door, or at the end of a night, there was something pure Dublin about it for her. *Go in good health* and *Get lost* all at once.

—Sorry to hear about your trouble.

—Don't worry, Dad, I'll crush her.

Crush her? Really? There's no doubt that Elliot has, and could, crush many a thing, though perhaps he shouldn't wear it as a badge of honor. The big rich white man crushing the small brown girl? Hardly a moment of enlightenment. No rewriting of history. How many times has that happened, from Christopher Columbus all the way here, now, to Elliot Mendelssohn?

—Just look after yourself, son.

Which is not what he meant to say at all. Rather he should

have said: Don't be despicable, Elliot. Stop twisting women's arms. Display some heart. Stop whining. Show some character. Grow up. Talk to me about our gone days. Give me something to kvell over.

Elliot leans down to sip the last of his wine, a trickle in the end of the glass.

And what is this but a hand coming across the table to shake his, as if they have just done a business deal, no stand-and-hug, no clap on the back, no manly peck on the cheek. Not quite sure, Elliot, if I've ever disliked you more than at this particular moment. Is that it? Is that all we get? No sweet words, no revelations, no human resolutions, just a new word added to the lexicon, and not even a good one.

Elliot swipes a napkin across his wine-colored mouth and throws the crumpled result down upon the table, a mountain of cloth.

—I'll call you.

—You do that.

—We'll get a proper lunch.

Gay gazinta hate indeed. Elliot, son, you could clear a room quicker than the Black Death.

There he goes, lumbering across the restaurant towards the coat check. Keying something again into his cursed phone. Stared at by Dandinho. He might burn a hole in his back. Go ahead, Dandinho, wrap him in aluminum and sling him out into the street.

—Rosita.

She turns immediately from the bar where she is leaning seductively against the counter.

—Yes, Mr. Mendelssohn?

—I think I'm finished here. Can you have Dandinho wrap them up? And I'd like to order a dessert.

—Yes, sir. What'll you have?

He should ask her now about her paintings. What is your life really like, out there in Brooklyn, or the Bronx, and that blue on your wrist, is that from a painted sky, because all I can remember of a very blue sky was a day in September when it all came crashing down.

—The tiramisu, I suppose.

—Great choice, Mr. Mendelssohn.

Thank you, my dear. Lovely once and always, moonlight in your hair. Time was, once, when the world was full of the likes of you.

And there the silhouette of Elliot goes, along past the window, the dark shaping itself into the white of the storm.

Jilted, then. By my own son.

And look at that. Two little puddles of rainwater on the floor beneath the table. All that's left of Elliot.

Which makes him think: time to tap a kidney.

He scoots the chair away from the table. And how is a man supposed to negotiate these other tables all sandwiched together? A slalom course. Hit the gates, zoom down the snowy mountain, watch out for patches of ice.

—How is everything, Mr. Mendelssohn?

Eagleton, the new manager. A long skinny drink. Awful complexion. Skin all rutted and scarred. It would hardly help to tell him the truth.

—Just fine, thank you. The salmon was delicious.

—Good.

—And the waitress.

A strange look on Eagleton's face. Oh, no, no, no. Not that she was delicious. No, no. Or not that she wasn't. Just a good waitress. Is what I meant. Not delicious.

—She's very charming.

—I'm very glad to hear that, Mr. Mendelssohn. Can I help you there?

—I'm fine, thanks. A quick visit.

He nods in the direction of the bathroom. Just standing up, he can feel the necessity. God, oh, God, there are times indeed when the winter gear would help on the slippery slope.

Through the tables he goes, tapping his cane on the ground. He flicks a quick look towards the kitchen through the circular porthole on the swinging kitchen door. Like ships, these restaurants. He can just about make out Dandinho, ahoy there, in full and animate conversation with a small little aproned man. Not fisticuffs but certainly a little wave bouncing between them.

A flash of eyes from the aproned man. Over Dandinho's shoulder. Hardly a hello either, what is the world coming to? Just jocular no doubt. Wonder if that's the man who prepared my salmon? Though he doesn't look like a chef. More like a porter.

Onwards, anyway. The smell of Clorox. Bathe me in it. Cleanse me.

No emporium of handles in this bathroom but at least it's clean and tidy. Only a quick whizz anyway. Root around, find the equipment, extinguish, wash your hands, be on your way, two minutes flat, make the fire-hose company proud.

In the corridor, he glances towards the kitchen once more. No sign of Dandinho or the aproned man. Around the corner, through the tables. Candles in daytime. Snow still out the window.

Tiramisu on the table, yes. The world restored. Thank you, Rosita. What we all need, from time to time, is a little pick-me-up.

XI

He rode over Connecticut
In a glass coach.
Once, a fear pierced him,
In that he mistook
The shadow of his equipage
For blackbirds.

In nearly all interrogation rooms, the camera is set up high in a corner: the cobweb cam. It is preferable to have a glimpse of the doorway—the truth is so often worn in the shape of arrival. The innocent walk in and sit straight down, perplexed, their hands joined together as if eager to be in prayer, but the guilty often pause for a second to look at the room and gauge it, searching for a hiding place, ready to defy their own knowledge of what has happened.

The furnishings of the room are designed so that there is nowhere to turn: the bareness itself is an accusation. Two or three chairs, near always wooden. A simple desk, generally one with a shallow drawer: no sense of heft or hidden things. In the drawer, a few sheets of paper and a simple pen. A two-way mirror on the far wall, plain, unadorned. Nothing to be used as a weapon: no folding chairs or glass or sharp pencils. No cups or coffee machines. No distracting posters on the walls. A carpet is unlikely, but if it exists, it's monotone. The baseboards painted the same color as the walls. The light is often fluorescent and hard, though there is sometimes a table lamp that the detectives turn on when the truth starts to emerge: it softens the light, takes away the edges, redeems the room.

The camera is positioned high enough that it is not the first thing seen, but those who pause in the doorway—so often the guilty—glance upward at it. There is much to be interpreted from the eye-flick: fear, defiance, insolence, disdain. Often they try to sit with their backs to the lens but the detectives are quick to redirect them to the other side of the table. The detectives count the amount of times their interviewees look up at the camera: the more they do so, the more likely they are to lie.

Others—so often the innocent—go immediately to sit down, as if they want to protect their truth, keep it tight, hold it in its own little universe for a while, put their arms around it. Theirs is a searing gaze into the lens: a mixture of plea and terror.

There are times the detectives leave the interviewees alone in the room. They watch, then, through the two-way mirror. It is nearly always the guilty who wave up at the camera: a fuck-you defiance. Some go to the corner underneath the camera to try to hide from it. In some stations there is a second camera set up in the opposite corner, though sometimes it is just a dummy, a second eye.

The room is nearly always sealed off from sound, though the camera itself is wired to pick up all noise. For backup the detectives also use a recorder.

When Pedro Jiménez is hauled in for questioning he displays a curious cocktail of innocence and guilt. He arrives in a suit jacket and blue shirt and white chef pants, a sad garage sale of a man, fifty-seven years old, a little isthmus of hair in the center of his forehead. He is thin, but gone a little to jowl, an autumn of skin upon him. He stands in the doorway and glances around but doesn't look up to the camera, rather turns toward the Latina detective as if beseeching her to make sense of the room. Her hair is dark, her eyes are dark, her clothes dark too. She wears a simple gold chain around her neck. She touches Pedro's elbow and guides him toward the seat at the bare wooden desk. She is followed moments later by another detective, a pale white loaf of a man who takes his chair to the end of the table. He places the chair backward, puts his chin on the rest, leans close.

Hemmed in, Pedro glances up at the camera as if he might be able to see his own reflection in the glass, then looks back down at his hands upon the tabletop. Surprisingly he pulls from his pocket a pair of reading glasses, though there is nothing in front of him to read.

When he perches the glasses on his nose he seems like a different man, not a scruffy dishwasher anymore but something of the disheveled librarian about him.

The female detective speaks to him at first in a Spanish that seems as if it has been scuffed and rolled on the streets of the city. The date, the time, the exact location of the interview. Is he aware, she asks, that their conversation is being recorded? He has not been arrested, but the word *yet* seems silently attached to the end of her sentence. She knows that he is a family man. She'd like to help him out. She's not interested in his immigration status. She is friends with a lot of people in the Costa Rican community, she is from the islands herself, born in the D.R., moved here when she was two years old. She is easy, chummy, open, her body turned sideways in the chair. She knows that he has a past but everybody has a past, isn't that right, Pedro? Pedro nods, a slight shine behind his spectacles. The detectives stop to whisper in English and then Pedro tells her that he understands perfectly, he'd be happy to do the interrogation in either language. She says that, yes, Rick, her partner, is a bit rusty. We appreciate it, Pedro, she says, we really do. Still, she maintains a lilt to her questions, as if her English has just swum through the Caribbean. She is interested in clean slates, she says. She avoids the word *murder*. It is an assault, a serious assault, a tragedy really. Is he aware of what happened? Yes. Has he heard anything come along the grapevine? No. Some people just lose it, you know? I suppose so. Did you ever lose it yourself, Pedro? No, I'm a quiet man, I live a quiet life. You live in Brooklyn, yes? Yes. Where? You know, Coney Island. What's it like living out there, Pedro? Gets windy sometimes. That's funny, gets windy, you hear that, Rick, it gets windy in Coney Island, Pedro's a comedian. I'm not trying to be funny, Mami. Just kidding, Pedro—so, how long you been working in the city? Twenty years. How long in Chialli's? Four. Four? Yes. Hard to look after a family on a dishwasher's salary? My wife, she's dead. You get by? I get by. You got a daughter? Yeah, Maria. Maria's married? She just got divorced, she's looking for a job. She got laid off? Yeah, she got laid off a couple of months ago. She got kids? Two. That's a tough life, Pedro, divorced, two kids, just got laid off, want some water, Pedro? No. You look like you might need a drink of water.

He adjusts the glasses on his nose. She leans forward, the male detective leans back. It is as if there is some sort of swinging pulse in the room, the bodies, like rhyme, dependent on one another.

So, I'd like to talk about the restaurant, Pedro. Whatever you want, Mami, I've got nothing to hide. You can't remember anything unusual happening that day, like anything to do between you and Dandinho, because we heard a thing or two, let's be honest, let's be fair here, Pedro, we heard you had a little bit of *puñetazos*? He glances upward at the camera but holds a pursed tightness to his lips, shakes his head, no, that argument with Dandinho, that was nothing, Mami, nothing, they have a *fútbol* pool among the employees, you know, a little betting gig, and there was a—what do you call it?—a question over a Corinthians game in Brazil, a dispute, just a bit of fun, nothing to it. Was there anything else Dandinho said to you? No. You sure? I'm sure. And where did you go then, Pedro? The bathroom. But isn't that the busiest time of day, the lunch shift, Pedro, what are you doing going to the bathroom then? I was taking a shit. You were taking a shit? Yes. That's all right, Pedro, everyone takes a shit, but are you sure that shit of yours didn't get any snowflakes on it? Snowflakes? Did you go out the employee exit by any chance, maybe to get a breather, Pedro, maybe to have a smoke? I don't smoke. But did you go out, maybe pick up your jacket, maybe pick up your hat, and take a little breather outside, through the employee entrance, out the steel door to Madison Ave? I didn't go anywhere. Just went back to washing dishes? Yeah. Pearl diving they call it, isn't that right, Pedro? I suppose. Why do they call it pearl diving? Listen, I've got a job, I've got two grandkids, I don't know.

There is, in the questioning, a moving cadence, sometimes delivered to the point of the desired information, at other times looping in discursive swirls, designed precisely to disguise.

That's something we wanted to talk to you about, Pedro. What? About Maria. Maria? You know, her getting divorced, losing her job, coming back in to live with you in Coney Island. She wanted to save money. Did it put some pressure on you maybe? No. Because Maria, she had a good job—where was it she worked again?—what was it she said to us, Rick? You talked to Maria? Of course, we talked to Maria. Maria's got nothing to do with any of this. Any of what? What are you doing talking to

Maria? Any of what, Pedro? Nothing. Nothing? She's a good girl, is all I said. Of course, she's a good girl. Then leave her out of it. To be honest, Pedro, well, she had a lot of things to say. Maria wouldn't say nothing bad about me. Of course, she didn't say anything bad about *you*, she's crazy about you, *la niña de sus ojos*. So what's the problem? No problem, Papi. Then what am I doing here? You know the Barner Funds? The what? Maria was working for the Barner Funds. Yeah, what about it? What do you think of the Barner Funds? She had a good job, she liked it there, that's all. That's all? That's it. It didn't piss you off, Pedro? No, why should it? Even when she got fired? That's a couple of months ago, I told you. What do you think about the bosses there, Pedro? Nothing, none of my business, never thought about them. Because Maria told us that she was bringing a lawsuit against the Barner Funds for wrongful dismissal, did you know that? Sure. And what did you think? *Bueno,* no big deal. And you know that guy Elliot Mendelssohn? Huh? He's the son of the guy that got punched outside your restaurant? Yeah. You've got to forgive me here, Pedro, but this guy Elliot, he might've, I don't know, he might've *stepped* in between Maria and your son-in-law a few months ago. I don't know what you're talking about. You know what I mean, before she got fired? What? That's just what we heard, that he might've just had a bit of a wandering hand with Maria, that they—sorry to say this, Pedro, you're a father, and fathers don't like to hear this shit, mothers don't either, trust me, but fathers for sure don't, right? What the fuck. What I'm saying, Pedro, is they made *further acquaintance* a couple of times in a hotel in Stamford, where this guy Elliot lives, up there in Connecticut, with his wife and kids, he's got a fondness for hotels, Pedro, do you know what I mean, are you hearing me, Pedro, is anybody home, knock-knock, who's there, are you hearing me, Pedro, is anyone there? I don't know what you mean. You don't? No, I don't. Maybe you felt something bad about the Barner Funds, like maybe this guy Elliot was exploiting her, maybe he was dabbling a little too much? Maria never did that, Maria's a good girl, Maria was *married*. Don't get me wrong, Pedro—this guy Elliot he's a prime-rib asshole, we know that. I don't know him, never met him. Maybe he was suggesting to Maria that he was going to make her rich, but then he turns around and fires her? I said, I don't know what you're talking about. Maybe he was whispering sweet nothings. I never heard of him before. Maybe the jury'll buy that story, Pedro? What story? You being a father and all, you punched his father? I didn't punch no one. Are you sure about that, Pedro? I swear to God, Mami. You can call me Carla. I didn't punch no one. Maybe you didn't mean to hit him so hard, just an accident, like? I told you, I didn't touch him. Maybe pushed him over? No. You want that glass of water now? Are you telling me that I need a lawyer? Look, we're not trying to nail you here, Pedro. I have the right to a lawyer, I know that. You certainly do, but what we're trying to do is help you here, that man who died, he was a judge once, Pedro, Brooklyn Supreme Court, and the way things are looking, you're going to need *us* on your side. I didn't punch no one. 'Cause, me and Rick here, we're on your side.

It is then they must pause and change the tempo—not a good idea to walk out of the room and leave Pedro alone, in case he decides to clam up further, or engage a lawyer, but it is time to shift the territory a little, so Carla rises from her chair, leaving Pedro alone with Rick, the big damp white loaf, making the room so very male and somehow even more cramped. And it is here that Rick employs the direct gaze, the lean forward, the half-menace, and asks Pedro if he can explain again where he was at the time of the assault, and why did he move from his dishwashing station, and what was the earlier argument he had with Dandinho, and when he went to the bathroom is it possible that he took the employee exit to the street—can you answer me that, Pedro?—and is it possible perhaps he even ducked back in the same door just seconds later, is any of that viable at all, because it's understandable, man, it's his son, it's your daughter, you know what I mean? We're here to help, frankly I'd like to put that Elliot asshole behind bars, he's the one who should take the rap, know what I'm saying?

When Carla returns she has one glass of water and three orange sodas in glass bottles, and she slides the Jarritos across the table, and it is as if they are in a distant cantina together, somewhere safe and warm, somewhere they can trust one another, but Pedro leaves the soda sitting in front of him. Carla leans forward and asks again about Maria, what she was like growing up, if she had any problems, if she ever mentioned any difficulties at work, if she got upset, if she said anything about going to Connecticut. Pedro takes the water, but leaves the soda untouched.

The time slips away from them, the clockhands on the wall turn, the fluorescent light in the office remains constant. The detectives ready themselves for their last-line flurry.

So, Pedro, did she tell you? Tell me what? About her *thing* with Elliot Mendelssohn? Her *what?* Her liaison, you know, her monkey business. Don't know what you're talking about. How do I say it delicately for you, Pedro? Say what? She was fucking this guy, Pedro, now calm down, Papi, calm down, *cálmese*. I'm calm, don't talk about my girl that way. Okay, okay, what do you know about their *re-la-tion-ship?* I don't know nothing about that. Because the way I see it, she was living a good life, wasn't she, Pedro, at one stage, she was happy, right? I got nothing to say. She was a good girl, doing a good job, went to secretarial school, got a good husband, he was a nice guy, second generation, she's making you proud, you like your son-in-law, you like your grandkids, life is good, she's happy, she's got herself a little place in Rockaway, picket fence, you know what I mean, the American dream, are you there, Pedro, we gotta play knock-knock again? I'm listening. Working for an investment firm, wearing nice clothes, making some good money, assistant to the CEO, and here she is, now, she's working in Midtown, an office on Lexington Avenue, big glass tower, and then one day, poof, it's all gone, in a flash of smoke, her boss turns out to be the asshole he always threatened to be, and he flat-out fires her. I don't know nothing about that. And then you hear that he's in the restaurant? I didn't hear nothing. Maybe Dandinho tells you? Dandinho didn't tell me nothing. You're just talking *fútbol*? That's it. Dandinho, he's your best friend, right? What's Dandinho got to do with this? And you've confided in him maybe, about how your little girl lost this job at the Barner Funds, and he puts two-and-two together, says the old man is out there right now—Pedro, is that what happened?—because it's perfectly forgivable, man, I can see it plain as day, by the time Dandinho tells you that Elliot Mendelssohn is in the restaurant, he's gone, and you, you been washing his dishes. We were arguing about *fútbol*. But it's not just *fútbol*, is it, Pedro? Huh? Are you a baseball fan, Pedro? *Sí, claro*. What's your team? Don't really have one. So, how much do you get paid again, Pedro? Eight bucks an hour, ten-fifty for overtime. Not a great job, dishwashing, is it? It's okay, I do some other things too. Like what, Pedro? Some vending, you know. Is that right? Yeah. You push the peanuts then, do you, Pedro? I don't know what you mean. Where do you do your vending? At the Cyclones. You mean the *Brooklyn* Cyclones? Yeah, the Brooklyn Cyclones, what's the problem? And by any chance do they give you a uniform to wear, Pedro, a hat maybe? Sure, I wear a hat sometimes, everyone wears a hat, in the kitchen anyway, you got to wear a hat. But you wear a Brooklyn Cyclones hat? I don't know what you're talking about, Mami.

Slowly they draw back their words, form them into a fist, hold them in mid-air a moment, then propel them forward.

Because we got a guy on camera wearing a Brooklyn Cyclones hat and he looks like a dead ringer for you.

Where?

Outside Chialli's, leaning over the dead man.

I don't know nothing about it.

On camera, Pedro. A dead ringer.

For me?

You and him, Pedro, *dos gotas de agua*.

XII

The river is moving.
The blackbird must be flying.

More to the point, the endless journey home. Let freedom ring, Sally, from the hilltops. Throw another log on the fire. Warm the pan, boil the milk, melt the chocolate, position the chair, unfold the blanket, hear the lumber hiss. Perhaps I should call her and let her know I'm on my way. Then again, she'll probably rush out into the storm. What in the world are you doing, Mr. J.? I'm coming home, Sally. Jilted by my very own son. He left me high and dry. Not even dry, come to think of it. I could have done with some winter gear. He even let me pay the check. Still, we've a little salmon and a lot of steak to see us through the storm. Unwrapped for some reason. Dandinho didn't do his job.

Awkward this, having to hold the plastic bag and the walking stick at the same time. But here we go, onwards, upwards, away.

Well, almost.

He stands in the outer foyer and hears the restaurant door close behind him. *Goodbye now, Mr. Mendelssohn.* Her sweet Rhodesian Zimbabwean voice and the last strain of music from inside. Should hurry back in and order myself a hot brandy. A spoonful of sugar to help the medicine go down.

Good God, but it is curtaining down. Never seen anything quite like it. Slantways, broadside, edgeways. A theater, a block-buster, an opera of snow. All the taxi drivers onstage, sliding left, right, sideways into the pit. An applause of windshield wipers. Trucks and vans, headlights blazing, and some poor idiot on a motorcycle. An actual biting snow. Like those little circular weapons, a million flying *chakri* aimed my way.

Hardly a soul on the street. A tad early for the mommies and the nannies on their way down to PS 6. No flowerboys. No de-liverymen. No one shoveling. No rock-salt rollers.

Should hail a taxi, really, but he would have to take me past the synagogue, up to Eighty-eighth, down the block, back down Park Avenue, along Eighty-sixth again, and who knows what sort of trafficjam there might be in that direction. Car horns blaring everywhere. A terrible sound, really. Isn't the snow sup-posed to deaden the sound? How is it that my hearing gets worse but the awful sounds get louder day after day? A cacophony. That's the word. The pianist playing the contrabass. The sax-man on the violin. The flautist on the horn, so to speak.

Isn't there supposed to be a fine for overuse? Listen up, El-liot. They have it for car horns, they'll get you yet.

What is it that happened to him? Why couldn't he be the boy he promised he would be? He did well in his final exams, threw his graduation hat in the air, took his mother by the arm, walked her proudly around Cambridge. She was happy then, she laughed, we did, together. Moved back to the city. Lived in the Village. Found himself a little French girl. What was her name? So long ago now. Chantal. And she could. Sing, that is. Eileen was a big fan. A voice like a wren. At the holiday parties she was always there. And then she wasn't. A ladle dipping down into the well of the mind. The strangest things appear and disappear. Who was it who gazed into the bottom of the well? Who was looking for their reflection in the dark?

Dark it is too. For this time of day. But onwards, let's go.

A chill at the neck. Didn't even button up my coat properly. Spent so long inside sliding my arms into the sleeves, they must have felt they were getting me in a straitjacket. Still, they were happy, all of them. Left a ten-dollar bill for a sulky Dandinho, and gave Rosita thirty percent, why not, she deserves a thing or two beyond the blue mark on her wrist.

A beauty.

Reminded me somewhat.

As all beauty does.

He balances precariously against the wall of the foyer, shifts the collar and lifts the scarf out and over his mouth. An impromptu balaclava.

Here, Eileen, come take my hand and step me out onto Madison. Many days we walked here together, though I remember you in sunshine, you wore a pale sundress and a simple pearl necklace, though the truth is we probably remember things as more beautiful than they actually were. The years put a few pounds on her in the end, and she walked with a bit of a lopsided limp. The folds and the creases and the humps at the hip. Cruel, the way God plays it. The more we know of time, the less we have of it. The less we have, the more we want. The scales of justice. If there is such a word. I was born in the middle of something or other.

On now. Soldier forth.

Sally too.

Out into the hard bite of snow, one step, two. An immediate chill against the high of his cheeks. He closes his eyes and tries to shake the burn away. The shock of it. The wind and the storm wrapping itself around him. He stops to adjust the precarious leftovers. How quickly we step from one state to the other. Can't be much beyond two o'clock and it's already pitch-black. The dark rises from the ground and wings itself up.

—Elliot Mendelssohn.

Yes. No. Of course not. Question or statement? Who's to hear a thing when the goddamn car horns are going and the wind is howling and your scarf is up around your ears and the city is in uproar and there's still a symphony in your head from the restaurant, it's simply impossible to hear anything at all, but was that my name? Am I my son? Surely not. Not in this lifetime at least. The voice seems to come from behind and he turns to look over his shoulder, his tongue flickering against the wool scarf. Am I the son of my son? A better question. Though not one I'd like to answer right now.

Get me out of this storm, please. Good God, it's cold, and the snow stings and I can hardly see a thing, but there's no voice from behind at all, just the orange light of Chialli's catching the snowflakes and the footprints of others who have gone on before me.

Should have called Sally.

He turns slowly and the tip of the walking stick crunches in the soft snow. He slides his right foot around and follows, inch by inch, with the left, careful now, no handles along Madison, more's the pity, two glasses of Sancerre rolling through me, and who is this spectacle striding up to me now, deep brown eyes behind spectacles and a little spray of grayish hair from the baseball cap, who, leaning forward, a shade this side of homeless, maybe looking for a few shekels, though something vaguely familiar about him, who, and why in the world do his eyes have that shine, where is that coming from, how many faces have I seen like his, they were out there in Brooklyn for so many years, the hustlers the haters the barkers the bakers the shoeshine boys the two-bit conmen from every corner of the globe, but he knows my name, or my son's name at least, and maybe something has happened to Elliot, he might have slipped in the snow, hurt his back, or landed soft on his wallet, who knows, he didn't, after all, pay for lunch.

A twitch in the man's face like he's been carrying something and just let it drop, and then picked it up again and there again, someone's lived in that face a long hard time, I can recognize, that, and what is it I can do for you, young man, though he is not young at all, maybe forty, fifty, who can tell anymore?

No more than three steps away and something indeed has got the man's goose or his gander or his goat or whatever they call it. Hat pulled down just a little bit farther and I can't even see the shape of his eyes anymore. Mouth in a snarl, but something gentle, too, about that face, a chub to it—is that Tony?—it looks like Tony, off the door, what in the world did I do wrong with Tony, my stupidities, my Kan, my Kant—what is wrong with you, Tony?—did something happen to Sally perchance, has she sent you out in the snow to rescue me, Saint Bernard, where's your brandy, I thought about that just a moment ago, and why in the world are you striding up to me so fast, Tony, without your doorman clothes, without your gloves even, and your knuckles shiny brown, I have never seen you in your street clothes, did I not tip you enough at holiday time, did I say something errant a little while ago, one of my silly phrases, there are many, my head is an avalanche, and still he keeps coming, his shoulders rolling around in his dark jacket, he's small and he's boxy, an odd look for Tony—

Once, long ago, I skated on a frozen lake with knifeblades attached to the bottom of my shoes—

A single step away, but maybe that's not Tony at all, is it, not enough of the chub, and a bit on the short side, muttering something in Spanish now about my father, or his father, or someone's father, what in the world has gotten into the man, someone help me, now, what's he saying, the snow blowing hard around us, a cyclorama, and it's impossible to hear what the man is shouting, spittle coming from his mouth, his own little snow-storm, rapidfire, how many words do they have for it, leaning forward, oh the hat on my head shifting, but what is that you're saying, man, I can't hear a word in the thunderous roar, calm yourself down, hold on one second, you don't look a bit like Tony at all, who are you, where are you from, where have I seen you before, and oh the leftovers are shifting that's my son's name you're shouting my treacherous son you are unaproned and oh all over the street that white coming down not even the snow can stand up straight and oh—

The canal was easily the best place to cannonball.

It was evening all afternoon.
It was snowing
And it was going to snow.
The blackbird sat
In the cedar-limbs.

If it had been another day—without the snow, the wind, the early dark—they would have seen him fall like a character out of an old epic, all hat and history.

It would have been captured from the traffic-cam atop the ornate limbs of the lightpole on Eighty-sixth Street. Even in a low-definition download, he would have emerged from the restaurant, his scarf looped around his neck, and the hat perched rakishly. He would have stopped to adjust his overcoat and then he would have stepped forward on his walking stick. In the picture he would have accepted the punch and he would have stood stockstill a moment, as if registering its seismic quality. The blow would have landed in the middle of his chest. The knees of his trousers would have started to accordion, his legs would have pleated and the lower scaffold of his body would have begun to totter as if on delay. It would have taken a second or two for the puppetry to achieve full motion: the swoon, the dip, the crumble. His body would resign and he would keel over, all eighty-two years of him, disintegrating downward. They would see the ancient Homburg staying on his head for most of the fall, defying physics, the bag of leftovers from his lunch leaving his grip almost immediately, opening with a thump against the ground, the same time as his head cracks off the pavement. It would capture, too, the shape of the assailant standing on the street having just delivered the punch, momentarily frozen in place, unsure of what has happened in front of his eyes, looking down at his fist, then stuffing his hand into the pocket of his puffy jacket, walking quickly ten steps north, confused, then furtive, pulling the brim of his hat down farther, stepping into a shadowed entrance, opening the heavy metal door. A slice of anonymity dissolving into a further anonymity. The street would be quiet for just a moment, and then the busboy and the manager and the waitress would appear over the prone body on the street, and baby carriages would move along the avenue—more of them of course, if there had been no snow, no wind, no dark—and there could, then, have been eyewitnesses from the neighboring shops or from passersby to attest to the man stepping in and out of the entrance.

As it was, it was like being set down in the best of poems,

carried into a cold landscape, blindfolded, turned around, un-blindfolded, forced, then, to invent new ways of seeing.

It could have been, too, that had the camera angles in the restaurant been tilted in another direction, they might have seen Pedro Jiménez come in through the door, with sprinkles of snow on his shoulders, his hat whisked off and folded into his pocket, the jacket hung on a metal hook near the door. In that instance they might have seen Pedro return to the jacket just seconds later and tuck it under several dry coats in order to hide the wetness of his own. He could also have been seen shoving the baseball cap farther into the pocket. It might have been possible to catch him, just before he turned the corner toward the bathroom, stopping and putting the heels of his hands to his anguished face and pulling his skin tight, shaking his head quickly from side to side, as if to disperse the past few minutes from his life before he went back to his dishwashing station. Another angle might have shown the terror on his face, later in the afternoon, as specifics emerged from the chef, the manager, the waitresses, and the cops together huddled in the kitchen while he washed the pan that had grilled Mendelssohn's salmon. It might have shown the glances that went between him and Dandinho when the cops pulled Pedro aside for questioning, or the look on Dandinho's face by the front door, or the backglances both men gave when they left the restaurant late in the evening, checking out the angles of the camera by the front foyer at a time when the cops had already downloaded the footage for examination.

None of this was yet apparent: the homicide, like the poem, had to open itself to whatever might still be discovered.

The cops could have downloaded the footage from the subway station that night where the two men stood, sullen, waiting for the 4 train to take them home to Brooklyn. But who could have intuited what their silence meant? Who could have foretold what Dandinho might say to Pedro? Who could have guessed that they might have struck a pact together? Who could have interpreted Pedro's face as he got off the F train in Coney Island almost two hours later and pushed his way through the silver turnstile? Who could have understood his terror as he passed by the bodega on Tenth Street? Who could have known what thoughts rifled through him as he paused on the corner of Coney Island Avenue, then turned south toward the water? Even if we had access to the cameras that are peppered along the boardwalk, who could properly say that the man stuffing the puffy jacket and baseball cap in the garbage can was truly guilty? What can be seen from the manner in which he looks at the discarded clothes that nobody will ever find? What can be learned from the manner he walks away? What can be intuited from the way he gazes out to sea? What country lies out there? What past? Who is to know how much failure is still trembling through his fist?

Or maybe this is not the case at all. Maybe he is triumphant. Maybe he is raw with joy. Maybe he feels strong and justified. Perhaps he did this to avenge his daughter and her children, their poverty, their sadness, their loss of their father, the sins of their mother. Perhaps there is something entirely congratulatory in the way he walks back down the boardwalk, past the carnival grounds, under the twinkling lights. Perhaps he feels that he should do the same with the son of the man he killed. Perhaps he is thinking, Fuck you, Elliot Mendelssohn, you're next.

It is happening, as the poet says, and it is going to happen.

Pedro will be arrested six days later. He will be charged. He will plead not guilty. His daughter will make bail for him. The State will offer. Pedro will not take it. The State says it will go all-out: second-degree murder. Pedro's lawyer will say he should take a lesser charge, manslaughter perhaps, but Pedro will say no, he is too old for jail, he would rather fight it. He will go to trial almost a full year later. It will be up to a jury to decide. In a high-ceilinged room on Centre Street in lower Manhattan they will weigh it all up. Sift through the evidence. Disregard. Reinstate. A form of excavation and rebuilding. They will look for the one moment of revelation that might eventually turn to truth.

There will be doctors and paramedics and cardiologists and blunt-trauma experts, one who will say that Mendelssohn was killed by the punch, another who will say that he died when his head hit the ground. There will be two forensic video analysts who will ask for the courtroom curtains to be drawn. They will carefully analyze the footage for the jury using six flat screens: one for the judge, one for the prosecution, one for the defense, three for the jury. They will discuss compression, resolution, blurring, time stamps, frame rates, comparative analysis. They will show the angle of the fall. They will point out the brief appearance of the assailant. They will crop in and zoom out. They will focus on the cap and the jacket. They will argue about unique characteristics, the known and the unknown. They will not be able to show a recognizable face. They will, however, show the footage of the kitchen argument of Dandinho and Pedro. They will count through the minutes and seconds of Pedro's bathroom visit. They will show Pedro returning to the giant sinks beneath the Brooklyn Cyclones poster. They will freeze him there a moment, plunging his hands into warm water.

Are those hands cold? Are those hands tormented? Are those hands simply doing their chores?

The prosecution will call on Elliot Mendelssohn to testify. He will tighten his jacket and stride to the front of the courtroom, then slide into the witness box. He will try earnestness, rage, prolonged silence, even tears, but the judge will cut him short. His voice will crack on cross-examination. He will say he never met the accused in his life. He will showcase his habit of raising his forefinger when answering a question. A little tremble will animate his neck. He will say that the death of his father has left him bereft. He will look at his hands as if to check that what he just said was correct. He will say that he will never recover from the shock. He will plead and cajole. He will glance once at Pedro, then quickly away. He will step down from the dock with two ovals of sweat appearing even through the cloth of his jacket. At the rear of the Centre Street courtroom he will look at his cell phone as if the answers to all the questions can be found there.

The days will go on.

They will call on the restaurant manager, Christopher Eagleton, and the waitress, Rosita Oosterhausen. Rosita's testimony will be curt and polite. She will say that she helped Mendelssohn into his coat at the door. She will say that he was a sweet old man, and she has no idea who would choose to hurt him, or why. She will say that the trauma made her give up her job. She will say that she never saw such a pointless death. She will step down from the witness stand, furtive, coiled, as if embarrassed by her testimony. She will flick a quick look at Pedro, though he will not return her glance. Christopher Eagleton will appear nervous, as if anything he might say will affect the business of his restaurant. He will loosen his tie and say that he is very sorry for the loss of his favorite customer and he really has no clue why the attack might have occurred. He was present in the restaurant, yes, and he heard a commotion outside. He ran out to help, but did not see the assailant, or even the shape of the assailant, and really there was little more that he could say. He bent down to Mendelssohn, who appeared already dead. It all seemed entirely senseless to him. Certainly he never heard Pedro say an errant word about anyone, least of all Mendelssohn. He will leave the witness stand, head bowed, fists thrust into his jacket pockets.

The court will be told that the whereabouts of Dandinho are

unknown, he is thought to be in Rio de Janeiro with a wife and three children, although it is also possible that he was spotted working in a restaurant in Toronto, and he may also have been seen in a barbecue restaurant in South Carolina. They will hear that all attempts to contact him after the initial interrogations were impossible. The defense will claim that without Dandinho there is no case. The prosecution will say that the evidence is clear-cut, and Dandinho clearly aided in the crime, underlined by his subsequent disappearance. The court will call on Sally James who will have just returned from Tobago for a week with her nephew to settle her financial affairs. She will be polite and confused and she will carry a little handkerchief to dab her eyes. They will call on Maria Casillias who will testify to the fact that, yes, she is currently in the process of bringing a multimillion-dollar lawsuit against the Barner Funds, though settlement is imminent. She will say that, yes, she told her father about losing her job. She will admit that, yes, she mentioned Elliot's name. But she will say that, no, she never told him of the affair. And she will say that he never displayed any anger, she has never seen him raise a fist to anyone, least of all an old man, there is simply no way her father could have done such a thing. She will say that it's much more likely that Elliot came out of the snow and punched his own father, he is that sort of man. The court will hear an objection. She will say that, even if it wasn't Elliot, the old man probably slipped, that is the logical thing, it was snowing, can't you see that he slipped, didn't they say he had two glasses of wine? The judge will instruct her, quietly, to limit her emotions. She will step down from the stand, glancing at her father, and then turn away when her ex-husband emerges from the gallery to hold her hand.

The court will call on Pedro who, on his attorney's advice, will not testify. He will sit in the courtroom, stone-faced, gentle, unmoving, a hard man to read. The jurors will wait and they will listen. They will weigh up notions of truth and lies—the truth with its border emptiness, and lies with their standard narrative conventions. They will trawl through the vast compendium of facts and figures and conjecture. It will be, to them, like trying to mine for light in the darkness, working in shafts, pockets, seams, chutes. The judge will instruct the jury members of their responsibilities and they will retire to deliberate. They will watch—once again—the footage of Mendelssohn's fall outside the restaurant. They will watch, too, the footage of Pedro and Dandinho in the kitchen. They will ask to see it again and again: each time it appears to them differently. They will freeze Mendelssohn in midfall and that image itself will become the screensaver upon their imaginations: they will wake with it for many days, weeks, even months afterward.

Twelve days of testimony, then the verdict. It is captured on video of course. A high angle designed not to include the faces of the jurors. The wood-paneled room is airy and spacious. The judge is seated high at the front. The Star-Spangled Banner on one side of him. The New York State flag on the other. The court reporter to the judge's right. The lawyers set up on opposite sides of each other. A sense that the room has been here forever, set down in aspic, a place that will never change.

There is a courtroom window right behind Pedro Jiménez. When he stands, he blocks out some of the light. The lens takes a moment to adjust. It flares and comes back into focus. His head is bowed. His hands are clasped at his waist. His suit is a hopeful blue. He waits as the jury forewoman steps forth. He closes his eyes while pronouncement is read out.

The sky outside is an immense sheet of gray. There is no movement in the clouds at all.

More cameras in the city than birds in the sky.

WHAT TIME IS IT NOW,
WHERE YOU ARE?

1

He had agreed in spring to write a short story for the New Year's Eve edition of a newspaper magazine. An easy enough task, he thought at first. In late May he settled down to sketch out a few images that might work, but soon found himself struggling, adrift. For a couple of weeks in early summer he cast about, chased ideas and paragraphs, left a few hanging, found himself postponing the assignment, putting it to the back of his mind. Occasionally he pulled his notes out again, then abandoned them once more.

He wondered how he would ever push into the territory of a New Year's Eve story—create a series of fireworks perhaps, drop a mirrored ball in a city, or allow snow to slowly scatter across the face of a windowpane?

All the beginnings he attempted—scribbled down in notebooks—wrote themselves into the dark.

2

In early summer he landed on the idea that he could perhaps defy his own notions of what a New Year's Eve story could achieve and tell a military tale, perhaps the portrait of a soldier somewhere far away, a young American, say, in a distant land. He could find himself, say, in a barracks on New Year's Eve in Afghanistan, the simple notion of a Marine—let's say a young woman, slightly exhausted by war, sitting on the edge of a valley, in the cold, surrounded by sandbags, in the vast quiet, looking eastward, under a steel mesh of stars, all silence, not even the thrup of machine-gun fire in the distance, the grim perimeter of the soldier's reality set against the possibility of what might be happening elsewhere, say, at home in South Carolina, say, a relentless suburb of no great distinction, say, a house gone slightly sour with the years, say, a broken drainpipe hanging down from the garage, say, a boy in the driveway, a young boy, in a striped shirt and torn jeans, with a bicycle lying forlorn at his feet, her brother, or her cousin, or perhaps even her son, yes, maybe her son.

3

Looking out into the Afghan night—although it would be better to be specific, and she could be facing the gothic dark of the Kerengal Valley, maybe even the ridge over Loi Kolay Village— she would draw herself into the savagery found at the outpost of every war, several layers of black pressing down on the already-dark mountains, an area where even the stunted trees might seem as if they want to step off the cliffs and hurtle themselves to the valley floor, the darkness made again more visible by the

layer of frost covering everything, the sandbags, the steel re-
bars, the machine gun, a Browning M-57, the impossible stretch
of distance, the enormity of black sky, with everything so cold
that the young Marine, let's call her Sandi, wears a balaclava
over her face, under her helmet, and the tip-ends of Sandi's eyelashes have frozen and her lungs feel thick with ice and when she
looks through the small gap in the sandbags her teeth chatter so
much that she is afraid she might chip them, a personal dread,
since Sandi is hipheavy and small-breasted and unpretty in her
own eyes, and twenty-six years old and feeling every single day
of it, but proud of her strong white teeth, so that when she takes
the upper lip of the balaclava and stretches it down across her
mouth, the fabric tastes hard and rough and synthetic against
her tongue.

4

Sandi sits alone in her rocky outpost. Unlikely of course, but he
knows a few Marines back in New York, and he has heard their
stories, and he is well aware that reality so often trumps inven-
tion, so he justifies her aloneness with the idea that a New Year's
Eve party is taking place in the village barracks below, and Sandi
has agreed to give the other Marines a break, that she will take
the post alone for an hour while midnight tips over, while the
ball drops distantly, because everyone in Sandi's unit knows that
Sandi is decent, Sandi is cool, Sandi knows the score, and, let's
be honest, Sandi likes her privacy, and she has been given special

access to a satellite phone that she can use at the stroke of midnight, since who wants to be alone on New Year's Eve without a way to at least call home and say—and what is Sandi going to say?

(He has, he must admit, no idea yet.)

What he does know is that the sense of cold seclusion is important: not only because it is a New Year's Eve story, but because it freezes Sandi in her cube of human loneliness, like most of us, at the unfolding of a year, looking backward and forward, both. Not only that, but the reader must begin to *feel* the cold that claws Sandi up there on the 308-meter ridge: so much so that she, or he, almost inhabits the very trees that want to step off the cliff. We should feel our own eyelashes freeze, and clench our cheeks to stop our own teeth chattering, because, like Sandi, we have something we must see, or understand, or at least imagine into existence, far away, and we, too, have a distant hope that Sandi will say something into her satellite phone, perhaps not a resolution, but at least a resolve of some sort, a small parcel of meaning.

(Though he still has little idea of what exactly she might say, she is beginning to become a little more complex for him, which he's grateful for, since deadline is approaching, he has to have it finished by mid-October at the latest, and he hunkers down for three or four days, in late September, in his apartment on Eighty-sixth Street in New York, though he can still somehow feel the cold seeping in from the Afghan hills, and he wants now to capture the essence of what it feels like to be far from home, to be in two or three places all at once, and the simple notion that what we really need on New Year's Eve is a sense of return, whether to his own original Dublin, or to Sandi's Charleston, or to his New York, or Sandi's birthplace which is, let's say, Ohio, though Sandi of course could be born just about any place, but Ohio feels right, let's say Toledo.)

5

This he now knows: Sandi Jewell is twenty-six years old, from Toledo, she lives in the south, she's a Marine, she perches in her camouflage more than 1,010 feet high in the debilitating cold, wearing a balaclava, looking out at the Afghan dark on the eve of the new year, about to dial a loved one on a satellite phone at her side. (He wonders what might happen if once, a year ago, there were three space heaters in the lookout, but they leaked out a light so that a sniper took out another Marine simply by lining up the shot in the center of the heaters, a perfect mathematical triangulation, an incident Sandi might have been aware of when she volunteered to take the outpost, adding another sense of dread to the story—perhaps it could happen again, a leak of light from her satellite phone this time? After a few days he decides against it—it would be far too simple to embrace the ease of death by sniperfire, and what sort of New Year's story might that be anyway?) The essence of Sandi's story has begun to place layers upon layers, though he does not know yet who the loved one is, or what might eventually exist between them. Still, a certain mystery has begun to join things together.

6

What Sandi sees, or what he imagines Sandi can see: the boy lays his bicycle down in the driveway, somewhere suburban, a Legoland of houses, on the outskirts of Charleston. It is midafternoon in mid-America, eight and a half hours behind Afghanistan. He is a tall, thin handsome boy. Let's say he is definitely her son (the desire to talk must be immense, and the potential for tragedy real: what might happen if she doesn't get to talk to him? What happens if the line goes dead? What happens if a shot rings out in the night?). He is fourteen years old, tricky, of course, since Sandi was earlier established as twenty-six years old. (Is he *really* her son? Is that feasible? Is it even possible?) The boy lifts the corrugated garage door, his heart thumping in his blue-and-white-striped shirt, and he hears a shout from inside the house, a woman (let's name her Kimberlee) trilling out to him (let's name him Joel) to say: *Quick, Joel, your mom's about to call.* And Joel is late, he knows he's late, and he's old enough now—almost fifteen in fact—to have a sweetheart and to know some things about the complexities of loss. He has spent an afternoon with her down there near the school bleachers on Lancaster Street. He has pledged himself to her, he will be with her later tonight when the real clock (the American clock) strikes midnight, but first he must talk to his second mother in Afghanistan from the kitchen of his first mother's house.

(And though Joel calls her his "second mother," and he has only known Sandi for four years, he has scrawled an ink tattoo inside his wrist, *K & S*.)

Joel hurries through the house, slings his jacket across the kitchen table, yanks up a chair, glances at Kimberlee, and says, while he stares at gaps in the hardwood floor: "What time is it now, where she is?"

7

Sandi sits in the dark, wearing a watch strapped to the outside of her wrist, over her tan Nomex fireproof gloves, waiting for the countdown. There have been problems with the phone signal in the past—dropped calls, endless ringing, failed satellites.

It is too early yet to call but she keys the phone alive anyway and touches the ridges of the numbers, a rehearsal.

Out beyond the outpost, nothing but the dark and the white frost on the land. The stars themselves like bulletholes above her.

8

He wants desperately to create gunfire across the Afghan hills, or to see a streak of light that is not just a metaphor—an RPG perhaps, or the zip of an actual bullet into one of the sandbags—to force a tracerline across the reader's brain, to ignite alternative fireworks on the eve of the new year, and to increase the intensity of the possible heartbreak.

But the simple fact is that the Afghan night remains quiet, no matter what he imagines, not even the howl of a stray dog, or the faint hint of voices in the outpost.

At two minutes to midnight Sandi drops the balaclava from between her teeth and leans across to pick up the satellite phone once more. (He has an inkling now of what she might say to her son, or rather Kimberlee's son.) Sandi clicks the flashlight on the front of her helmet, thumbs the phone on forcefully. The front panel lights up. She has been given a code. She takes off her gloves in order to dial the numbers precisely. She has a botched tattoo on the flap of skin between her thumb and forefinger, the initials of someone else's name from long ago, she does not think of him anymore.

It is midnight in Afghanistan and early afternoon in South Carolina.

9

He is writing this (almost) last part now in France where he is traveling after a book event. It is the middle of September and deadline is looming. Some things he knows for sure—Sandi will not die, she will simply pick up the phone, she will dial through, she will call her lover and her lover's son, and she will simply say, "Happy New Year," in the most ordinary way, and they will return the greeting, and life will go on, since this is what our New Year's Eves are about, our connections, our bonds, no matter how inconsequential, and the story will be quiet and slip its way into its own new year.

10

Inside the kitchen on North Murray Avenue, Kimberlee stands at the counter, with her hands webbed wide, waiting for the call. Spread out in front of her is the prospect of a feast—chopped peppers, onions, a half pound of oysters, a cup of cooked shrimp, tomatoes, sprigs of thyme, lemon, lime, olive oil, salt, three cloves of garlic for the bouillabaisse she has planned.

Kimberlee has placed a second wineglass at the end of the table. She is thirty-eight years old, tall, slim, pretty, a university professor. She aches for the call. She has not talked to Sandi in a week, since just after Christmas, when they argued about the length of Sandi's tour. The call itself has become a distant memory, a barely remembered pulse. Kimberlee listens to the wine gurgle against the side of the glass. This to her is the essence of the season: the loneliness, the longing, the beauty. She reaches for a spoon and begins to stir.

11

It's late September, and he is seriously deadlined now, but he is struck by the notion that the story is endless. He could stay with

Kimberlee, or he could return to Afghanistan, or he could slide into the past, or he could follow Joel down to the bleachers with his sweetheart later tonight (let's call her Tracey), or he could descend the hill to where the other Marines are having their party, or he could follow the path of a satellite, or he could go back to Sandi's original lover, or he could summon in the snow to swirl across the night.

He is in Normandy by the sea. The waves ribbon and buckle on the shores of Étretat.

12

He cannot get this phrase out of his mind: *The living and the dead.*

13

How is it that a particle of a voice gets transmitted down a telephone line? How is it that Sandi summons up a simple phrase, and the muscles in her throat contract? How is it that Kimberlee hears a sound and already her hand is moving through space to reach for the white kitchen telephone? How is it that Joel feels a pang of desire for Tracey? (What exactly will those bleachers look like at midnight?) (And who, by the way, is Joel's father?) (And what is it that Kimberlee teaches in university?) (Did she meet Sandi on a college campus?) (What might Sandi have been studying?) (When did Sandi move from Ohio?) (Did she join the Marines after a breakup?) (Was she married before she met Kimberlee?) (What is that initial tattooed on her hand?) (Does she want to have a child of her own?) How is it that a voice travels halfway around the world? Does it go through underwater cables, does it bounce off of satellites? How does a quark transmit itself to another quark? How many seconds of delay are there between Kimberlee's voice and Sandi's? Could a bullet travel that distance without them knowing? Could there now be a death at the end of this story? (Are there any female engagement teams in the Kerengal Valley?) (Is there even such a thing as a Browning M-57?) How private is the phone call? Who might be listening in? Can we create a brand-new character so late on, let's say an agent in Kabul, a malevolent little slice of censorship, eavesdropping in on Sandi? Can we see him there, with his headphones, his heartlessness, his bitterness, his rancor?

And what about his own childhood New Year's Eves in Dublin? Could he disappear back to them? What was that song his father used to sing? What about those days when he used to run out into the Clonkeen Road at midnight, banging saucepans to ring in the new year? What about that sense of promise the Januarys used to bring to his boyhood?

But more important—and perhaps most important—what happens to Sandi when she gets through on the telephone? What sort of feeling will rifle through her blood when she hears Kimberlee's voice? What great desire might arc between them? Or what sort of silence might hollow itself down the telephone line?

What will happen if they argue once again? Will Sandi describe the bunker where she sits? Will she try to articulate the darkness? Will those fine teeth chatter in the cold? Will Kimberlee open up immediately and make her young lover laugh? Will the white wine disappear from the glass? Will she talk about the bouillabaisse? Will she even use the word *love*? What will Joel's first words be to Sandi? Will he tell her about Tracey? Will he tell her that he will go down to the bleachers tonight? Will Joel's father (let's call him Paul, living up north, in a college town in New Hampshire, a biologist, an anti-war activist) ever hear any of this? How many years has he been estranged from Kimberlee? Has Sandi ever met him? How long will the phone call eventually last? What happens if the satellite suddenly fails?

Where will his own children be this New Year's Eve?

How do we go back to the very simplicity of the original notion? How do we sit with Sandi in her lonely outpost? How do we look out into the dark?

(And who, anyway, was that dead Marine?)

13 redux

The phone rings: it rings and rings and rings.

SH'KHOL

It was their first Christmas in Galway together, mother and son. The cottage was hidden alongside the Atlantic, blue-windowed, slate-roofed, tucked near a grove of sycamore trees. The branches were bent inland by the wind. White spindrift blew up from the sea, landing softly on the tall hedges in the back garden.

During the day Rebecca could hear the rhythmic approach and fall of the waves against the shore. At night the sounds seemed to double.

Even in the wet chill of the December evenings, she slept with her window open, listening to the roll of the water sounding up from the low cliffs, rasping over the run of stone walls, sweeping toward the house, where it seemed to pause, hover a moment, then break.

On Christmas morning she left his present by the fireplace. Boxed and wrapped and tied with red ribbons. Tomas tore the package open, and it fell in a bundle at his feet. He had no idea what it was at first: he held it by the legs, then the waist, turned it upside down, clutched it dark against his chest.

She reached behind the tree and removed a second package: neoprene boots and a hood. Tomas stripped his shoes and shirt:

he was thin, strong, pale. When he pulled off his trousers, she glanced away.

The wetsuit was liquid around him: she had bought it two sizes too big so he could grow into it. He spread his arms wide and whirled around the room: she hadn't seen him so happy in months.

Rebecca gestured to him that they would go down to the water in a few hours.

THIRTEEN YEARS OLD AND THERE was already a whole history written in him. She had adopted him from Vladivostok at the age of six. On her visit to the orphanage, she had seen him crouched beneath a swing set. His hair was blond, his eyes a pellucid blue. Sores on his neck. Long, thin scars on his lower back. His gums soft and bloody. He had been born deaf, but when she called out his name he had turned quickly toward her: a sign, she was sure of it.

Shards of his story would always be a mystery to her: the early years, an ancestry she knew nothing about, a rumor that he'd been born near a rubbish dump. The possible inheritances: mercury, radiation sickness, beatings.

She was aware of what she was getting herself into, but she had been with Alan then. They stayed in a shabby hotel overlooking the Bay of Amur. Days of bribes and panic. Anxious phone calls late in the night. Long hours in the waiting room. A diagnosis of fetal alcohol syndrome gave them pause. Still, they left after six weeks, swinging Tomas between them. On the Aeroflot flight, the boy kept his head on her shoulder. At customs in Dublin, her fingers trembled over the paperwork. The stamp came down when Alan signed. She grabbed Tomas's hand and ran him, laughing, through Arrivals: it was her forty-first birthday.

The days were good then: a three-bedroom house in Stepaside, a series of counselors, therapists, speech experts, and even her parents to help them out.

Now, seven years on, she was divorced, living out west, her parents were gone, and her task had doubled. Her savings were stretched. The bills slipped one after the other through the letter box. There were rumors that the special school in Galway might close. Still, she wasn't given to bitterness or loud complaint. She made a living translating from Hebrew to English—wedding vows, business contracts, cultural pamphlets. There was a literary novel or two from a left-wing publisher in Tel Aviv: the pay was derisory, but she liked stepping into that otherness, and the books were a stay against indifference.

Forty-eight years old and there was still a beauty about her, an olive to her skin, a sloe to her eyes, an aquiline sweep to her nose. Her hair was dark, her body thin and supple. In the small village she fit in well, even if she stood at a sharp angle to the striking blondness of her son. She relished the Gaeltacht, the shifting weather, the hard light, the wind off the Atlantic. Bundled up against the chill, they walked along the pier, amongst the lobster pots and coiled ropes and disintegrating fishing boats.

The rain slapped the windows of the shuttered shops. No tourists in winter. In the supermarket the local women often watched them: more than once Rebecca was asked if she was the *bean cabhrach,* a phrase she liked—the help, the nanny, the midwife.

There was a raw wedge of thrill in her love for him. The presence of the unknown. The journey out of childhood. The step into a future self.

Some days Tomas took her hand, leaned on her shoulder as they drove through the village, beyond the abandoned schoolhouse, past the whitewashed bungalows toward home. She wanted to clasp herself over him, shroud him, absorb whatever came his way. Most of all she wanted to discover what sort of man might emerge from underneath that very pale skin.

TOMAS WORE THE WETSUIT all Christmas morning. He lay on the floor, playing video games, his fingers fluid on the console. Over the rim of her reading glasses, Rebecca watched the gray stripe along the sleeve move. It was, she knew, a game she shouldn't allow—tanks, ditches, killings, tracer bullets—but it was a small sacrifice for an hour of quiet.

No rage this Christmas, no battles, no tears.

At noon she gestured for him to get ready: the light would fade early. She had two wetsuits of her own in the bedroom cupboard, but she left them hanging, pulled on running shoes, an anorak, a warm scarf. At the door Tomas threw his duffle coat loose around the neoprene.

—Just a quick dip, she said in Irish.

There was no way of knowing how much of any language Tomas could understand. His signing was rudimentary, but she could tell a thing or two from the carry of his body, the shape of his shoulders, the hold of his mouth. Mostly she divined from his eyes. He was handsome in a roguish way: the eyes themselves were narrow, yes, but agile. He had no other physical symptoms of fetal alcohol, no high brow, no thin lip, no flat philtrum.

They stepped out into a shaft of light so clear and bright it seemed made of bone. Just by the low stone wall, a cloud curtained across and the light dropped gray again. A few stray raindrops stung their faces.

This was what she loved about the west of Ireland: the weather made from cinema. A squall could blow in at any time and moments later the gray would be hunted open with blue.

One of the walls down by the bottom field had been reinforced with metal pipes. It is the worst sort of masonry, against all local tradition, but the wind moved across the mouths of the hollow tubes and pierced the air with a series of accidental whistles. Tomas ran his hand over the pipes, one by one, adjusting the song of the wall. She was sure his fingers could gauge the vibrations in the metal. Small moments like these, they crept up, sliced her open.

Halfway toward the water, he broke into a Charlie Chaplin walk—twirling an imaginary walking stick as he bent forward into the gale, feet pointed sideways. He made a whooping sound as he topped a rise and caught sight of the sea. She called for him to wait: it was habit, even if his back was turned. He remained at the edge of the cliff, walking in place. Almost a perfect imitation. Where had he seen Chaplin? Some video game maybe? Some television show? There were times she thought that, despite the doctors, he might still someday crack open the impossible longings she held for him.

At the precipice, above the granite seastack, they paused. The waves hurried to shore, long scribbles of white. She tapped him on the small of his back where the wetsuit bunched. The neoprene hood framed his face. His blond hair peeked out.

—Stay where it's shallow now. Promise me.

She scooted behind him on her hunkers. The grass was cold on her fingertips. Her feet slid forward in the mud, dropped from the small ledge into the coarse scree below. The rocks were slick with seaweed. A small crab scuttled in a dark pool.

Tomas was already knee-deep in the cove.

—Don't go any further now, she called.

She had been a swimmer when she was a child, had competed for Dublin and Leinster both. Rows of medals in her childhood bedroom. A championship trophy from Brussels. The rumor of a scholarship to an American university: a rotator-cuff injury had cut her short.

She had taught Tomas to swim during the warmth of the summer. He knew the rules. No diving. Stay in the cove. Never get close to the base of the seastack.

Twice he looked as if he were about to round the edge of the dark rock into the deeper water: once when he saw a windsurfer, yet again when a yellow kayak went swiftly by.

She waved her arms: Just no more, love, okay?

He returned to her, fanned the low water with his fingers, splashed it high around her, both arms in his Chaplin motion.

—Stop it, please, said Rebecca softly. You're soaking me.

He splashed her again, turned away, dove under for ten seconds, fourteen, fifteen, eighteen, came up ten yards away, spluttering for air.

—Come on, now. Please. Come in.

Tomas swam toward the seastack, the dark of his feet disappearing into the water. She watched his wetsuit ripple under the surface. A long, sleek shadow.

A flock of seabirds serried over the low waves in a taunt. Her body stiffened. She edged forward again, waited.

I have, she thought, made a terrible mistake.

She threw off her coat and dove in. The cold stunned the length of her, slipped immediately along her skin.

THE SECOND SHE CLIMBED from the water, she realized she had left her phone in the pocket of her jeans. She unclipped the battery, shook the water out.

Tomas lay on the sand, looking up. His blue eyes. His red face. His swollen lips. It had been easy enough to pull him from the cove. He hadn't struggled. She swam behind him, placed her hands gently behind his shoulders, pulled him ashore. He lay there, smiling.

She whipped her wet hair sideways, turned toward the cliff. A surge of relief moved along her spine when she glanced back: he was following her.

The cottage felt so suddenly isolated: the small blue windows, the bright half-door. He stood in a puddle in the middle of the floor, his lips trembling.

Rebecca put the phone in a bag of rice to soak up the moisture, shook the bag. No backup phone. No landline. Christmas Day. Alan. He hadn't even called. He could have tried earlier. The thought of him in Dublin now, with his new family, their tidy house, their decorations, their dramas. A simple call, she thought, it would have been so easy.

—Your father never even phoned, she said as she crossed the room.

She wondered if the words were properly understood, and if they were, did they cut to the core: *your father, d'athair, abba?* What rattled inside? How much could he possibly catch? The experts in Galway said that his comprehension was minimal, but they could never be sure; no one could gauge that depth.

Rebecca tugged the wetsuit zip and gently peeled back the neoprene. His skin was taut and dimpled. He laid his head on her shoulder. A soft whimper came from him.

She felt herself loosening, drew him close, the cold of his cheek against her clavicle.

—You just frightened me, love, that's all.

When darkness fell, they sat down to dinner—turkey, pota-
toes, a plum pudding bought from an organic food store in Galway. As a child in Dublin, she had grown up with the ancient
Hanukkah rituals. She was the first in her family to marry outside the faith, but her parents understood: there were so few
Jews left in Ireland anyway. At times she thought she should
rebuild the holiday routines, but little remained except the faint
memory of walking the Rathgar Road at sundown, counting the
menorahs in the windows. Year by year, the numbers dwindled.

Halfway through the meal they put on the party hats, pulled
apart the paper crackers, unfolded the jokes that came within. A
glass of port for her. A fizzy orange drink for Tomas. A box of
Quality Street. They lay on the couch together, his cheek on her
shoulder, a silence around them.

She cracked the spine on an old blue hardcover. Nadia Mandelstam.

Tomas clicked the remote and picked up the game stick. His
fingers flitted over the buttons: the mastery of a pianist. She
wondered if the parents had been gifted beyond the drunken-
ness, if one day they had looked out of high conservatory windows, or painted daring new canvases, or plied themselves in
some poetic realm, against all the odds—sentimental, she knew,
but worth the risk, hope against hope, a faint glimmer in the knit
of neurons.

Christmas evening slipped away, gradations of dark outside
the window.

At bedtime she read to him in Gaelic from a cycle of ancient Irish mythology. The myths were musical. His eyes fluttered. She waited. His turmoil. His anger. Night rages, the doctors called them.

She smoothed his hair, but Tomas jerked and his arm shot out. His elbow caught the side of her chin. She felt for blood. A thin smear of it appeared along her fingers. She touched her teeth with her tongue. Intact. Nothing too bad. Perhaps a bruise tomorrow. Something else to explain in the village store. *Timpiste beag*. A small accident, don't worry. *Ná bac leis*.

She leaned over him and fixed her arms in a triangle so that he couldn't bash his head off the wall.

Her breath moved the fringe of his hair. His skin was splotchy with small, dark acne. The onset of early adolescence. What might happen in the years to come, when the will of his body surpassed the strength of her own? How would she ever be able to hold him down? What discipline would she need, what method of restraint?

She moved closer to him, and his head dipped and touched the soft of her breast. Within a moment he was thrashing in the sheets again. His eyes opened. He ground his teeth. The look on his face: sometimes she wondered if the fear edged toward hatred.

She reached underneath the bed for a red hatbox. Inside lay a spongy black leather helmet. She lifted it out. *Kilmacud Crokes Are Magic!* was scrawled in silver marker along the side. Alan had worn it during his hurling days. If Tomas woke and began bashing again, it would protect him.

She lifted the back of his head and slipped it on, tucked back his hair and fastened the latch beneath his chin. Gently, she pried open his mouth and set a piece of fitted foam between his teeth so they wouldn't crack.

Once he had bitten her finger while asleep, and she had given herself two stitches—an old trick she had learned from her mother. There was still a scar on her left forefinger: a small red scythe.

She fell asleep beside him in the single bed, woke momentarily unsure of where she was: the red digits on the alarm shining.

The phone, she thought. She must check the phone.

She went to the fridge for a bottle of white wine, stoked her bedroom fire, put Sviatoslav Richter on the stereo, settled the pillows, pulled a blanket to her chest, opened the bottle and poured. The wine sounded gently against the glass, a kindling to sleep.

IN THE MORNING Tomas was gone.

She rose sleepily at first, gathered the blanket tight around her neck. A reef of light broke through the bare sycamores. She turned the pillow to the cool side. She was surprised by the time. Nine o'clock. The wine still lay on her breath, the empty green bottle on the bedside table: she felt vaguely adulterous. She listened for movement. No video games, no television. A hard breeze moved through the cottage, an open window perhaps. She rose with the blanket around her. The cold floor stung her bare feet. She keyed the phone alive. It flickered an instant, beeped, fell dead again.

The living room was empty. She pushed open the door of his room, saw the hanging tongue of bedsheet and the helmet on the floor. She dropped the blanket from around her shoulders, checked under the bed, flung open the cupboard.

In the living room, the hook where the wetsuit had hung was empty.

The top half of the front door was still latched. The bottom half swung, panicky in the wind. She ducked under, wearing only her nightgown. The grass outside was brittle with frost. The cold seeped between her toes. His name was thrown back to her from among the treetops.

The sleeves of grass slapped hard against her shinbones. The wind played its tune over the pipes in the stone wall. She spied a quick movement at the edge of the cliff—a hunched figure darting down and away, bounding along the cliff. It appeared again, seconds later, as if out of the sea. A ram, the horns curled and sharp. It sped away along the fields, through a gap in the bushes.

Rebecca glanced down to the cove. No shoes on the rocks. No duffle coat. Nothing. Perhaps he had not come here at all. Good God, the wetsuit. She should never have bought it. Two sizes too big, just to save money.

She ran along the cliff, peered around the seastack. The wind blew fierce. The sea lay silver and black, an ancient, speckled mirror. Who was out there? Maybe a coast-guard boat. Or an early-morning kayaker. A fishing craft of some sort. The wind soughed off the Atlantic. Alan's voice in her head. *You bought him what? A wetsuit? Why, for crying out loud?* How far might he swim? There were nets out there. He might get tangled.

—Tom-as!

Perhaps he might hear her. A ringing in his ears, maybe, a vibration of water to waken his eardrum.

She scanned the waves. Snap to. Pull yourself together for fucksake.

She could almost see herself from above as she turned back for the cottage: her nightdress, her bare feet, her hair uncoiled, the wet wind driving against her. No phone, no fucking phone. She would have to get the car. Drive to town. The Gardaí. Where was the station, anyway? Why didn't she know? Which neighbors might be home? You bought him what? What sort of mother? How much wine did you drink? Fetal alcohol.

The wind bent the grass-blades. She stumbled forward over the low wall, into the garden, a sharp pain ripping through her ankle. At the back of the cottage the trees curtsied. The branches speckled the wall with shadows. The half-door swung on its hinges. She ducked under, into his bedroom again. *Kilmacud Crokes Are Magic!*

Still the phone did not work.

At the kitchen counter she keyed the computer alive. The

screen flared—Tomas at six in Glendalough, blond hair, red shorts, shirtsleeves flapping as he sauntered through the grass toward the lake. She opened Skype, dialed the only number she knew by heart. Alan answered on the sixth ring. Jesus. What had she done? Was she out of her fucking mind? He would call the police, the coast guard, too, but it would take him three or four hours to drive from Dublin. Phone me when you find him. Hurry. Just find him. Fucksake, Rebecca. He hung up into a sudden, fierce silence.

When she closed Skype, the background picture of Tomas appeared once more.

She ran to her bedroom, struggled into her old wetsuit. It chafed her body, tugged across her chest, scraped hard against her neck.

A menace of clouds hung outside. She scanned the horizon. The distant islands lay humped and cetacean. Gray water, gray sky. Most likely he'd swum north. The currents were easier that way. They'd gone that direction in summer. Always close to shore. Reading the way the water flowed. Where it frothed against rocks, curved back on itself.

A small fishing boat trolled the far edge of the bay. Rebecca waved her hands—ridiculous, she knew—then scrambled down along the cliff face, her feet slipping in the moist track.

Halfway to the beach she stopped: Tomas's tennis shoes lay there, neatly pointed toward the sea. How had she missed them earlier? She would remember this always, she knew: she turned the shoes around, as if at any moment he might step into them and return, plod up to the warm cottage.

No footprints in the sand: it was too coarse. No jacket, either. Had he left his duffle behind? Hypothermia. It could come on within minutes. She had bought the wetsuit so big. He was more likely to be exposed. Where would he stop? How long was he gone now? She had woken so late. Wine. She had drunk so much wine.

She pulled a swimming cap hard over her hair and yanked the zip tight on her wetsuit. The teeth of it were stiff.

Rebecca waded in, dove. The cold pierced her. Her arms rose and rose again. She stopped, glanced back, forced herself onward. Her shoulder ached. She saw his face at every stroke: the dark hood, his blond hair, his blue eyes.

Out past the seastack, she moved along the coast, the sound of the waves in her ears, another deafness, the blood receding from her fingers, her toes, her mind.

A NOVELLA HAD ARRIVED from the publisher in Tel Aviv eight months before, a beautifully written story by an Arab Israeli from Nazareth: an important piece of work, she thought.

She had begun immediately to translate it, the story of a middle-aged couple who had lost their two children. She had come upon the word *sh'khol*. She cast around for a word to translate it but there was no proper match. There were words, of course, for *widow, widower,* and *orphan,* but no noun, no adjective, for a parent who had lost a child. None in Irish, either. She looked in Russian, in French, in German, in other languages, too, but could find analogues only in Sanskrit, *vilomah,* and in Arabic, *thakla,* a mother, *mathkool,* a father. Still none in English. It had bothered her for days. She wanted to be true to the text, to identify the invisible, *torn open, ripped apart, stolen.* In the end she had settled upon the formal *bereaved,* not precise enough, she thought, no mystery in it, no music, hardly a proper translation at all, *bereaved.*

IT WAS ALMOST NOON when she was yanked in by the neck of her wetsuit. A coast-guard boat. Four men aboard. She fell to the deck, face to the slats, gasping. They carried her down to the cabin. Leaned over her. A mask. Tubes. Their faces: blurry, unfocused. Their voices. Oxygen. A hand on her brow. A finger on her wrist. The weight of water still upon her. Her teeth chattered. She tried to stand.

—Let me back, she pleaded.

The cold burned inside her. Her shoulder felt as if it had been ripped from its socket.

—Sit still now, you'll be all right. Just don't move.

They wrapped her in silver foil blankets, massaged her fingers and toes, slapped her twice across the cheek, gently, as if to wake her.

—Mrs. Barrington. Can you hear me?

In the blue of the skipper's eyes she saw Tomas appear, disappear. She touched his face, but the beard bristled against her hand.

The skipper spoke to her in English first, then Irish, a sharpness to his tone. Was she sure Tomas had gone swimming? Was there any other place he might be? Had he ever done this before? What was he wearing? Did he have a phone? Did he have any friends along the coast?

She tried to stand once more, but the skipper held her back.

The wind buffeted the cabin windows, whitened the tops of the waves. A few gulls darted acrobatically above the water. Rebecca glanced at the maritime maps on the wall, enormous charts of line and color. A furnace of grief rose up in her. She peered out past the stern, the widening wake. The radio crackled: a dozen different voices.

She was making the sounds, she knew, of an animal.

The boat slowed suddenly, pulled into a slipway. A fine shiver of spray stung her face. She did not recognize the area. A lamplight was still shining in the blue daytime. A faint glow, a prospect of dark. Onlookers huddled by their cars, pointing in her direction. Beams of red and blue slashed the treetops. Rebecca felt a hand at her shoulder. The skipper escorted her along the pier. One of her blankets slipped away. She was immediately aware of her wetsuit: the tightness, the darkness, the cold. A series of whispers. She was struck by the immense stillness, the silence, not a breath of wind.

She turned, broke free and ran. *Sh'khol.*

When they pulled her from the water a second time, she saw a man hurrying toward her with his cell phone, watching the screen as he filmed her rising from the low, gray waves. He carried the phone like an accusation: she would, she knew, be on the Internet later that night.

—Tomas, she whispered as they put her in the car.

At home, a sedative dulled her. A policewoman sat in a corner of the room, silent, watching, a teacup and saucer in her hands. Through the large plate-glass window Rebecca could see figures wandering about, casting backward glances. One of them appeared to be scribbling in a notebook.

The Gardaí had set up in the living room. Every few moments another phone rang. Cars turned in the narrow laneway outside the cottage, their tires crunching on the gravel.

Somebody was smoking outside. She could smell a rag of it moving through the house. She rose to shut the bedroom window. Something has ended, she thought. Something has finished. She could not locate the source of the feeling.

She paused a moment and strode across the floor toward the bedroom. The policewoman uncrossed her legs but did not rise from the wicker chair. Rebecca strode out. The living room fell quiet, except for the static of a police radio. A wine bottle on the table. A discarded party hat. The scraps of their Christmas dinner heaped in the sink, swollen with dishwater.

—I want to join the search parties.

—It's best for you to stay here.

—He can't hear the whistles, he's deaf.

—Best stay in the cottage, Mrs. Barrington.

She felt as if she had chewed a piece of aluminum, the pain in her head suddenly cold.

—Marcus. My name is Marcus. Rebecca Marcus.

She pushed open the door of Tomas's room. Two plainclothes police were sifting through his cupboard drawers. On his bed was a small plastic bag marked with a series of numbers: strands of hair inside. Thin and blond. The detectives turned to her.

—I'd like to get his pajamas, she said.

—I'm sorry, Miss. We can't let you take anything.

—His jammies, that's all I want.

—A question. If you don't mind.

As the detective approached, she could smell the remnants of cinnamon on him, some essence of Christmas. He struck the question sharply, like a match against her.

—How did you get that bruise?

Her hand flew to her face. She felt as if some jagged shape had been drawn up out of her, ripping the roof of her mouth.

Outside, the early dark had taken possession of everything.

—No idea, she said.

A woman alone with a boy. In a western cottage. Empty wine bottles strewn about. She looked over her shoulder: the other guards were watching from the living room. She heard the rattle of pills from the bathroom. An inventory of her medicine. Another was searching her bookshelves. *The Iron Mountains. Factory Farming. Kaddish. House Beautiful. The Remains of the Day.* So, she was under suspicion. She felt suddenly marooned. Rebecca drew herself to full height and walked back toward the living room.

—Ask that person outside to please stop smoking, she said.

HE CAME DOWN THE LANEWAY, beeping the car horn, lowered the window, beckoned the guard over: *I'm the child's father.*

Alan had lost the jowls of his occasional drinking. The thinness made him severe. She tried to look for the old self that might remain, but he was clean-shaven, and there was something so deeply mannered about him, a tweed jacket, a thin tie pushed up against his neck, a crease in his slacks. He looked as if he had dressed himself in the third person.

He buried his face in Tomas's duffle by the door, then sank theatrically to his knees, but was careful to wipe the muck when he rose and followed her to her bedroom.

The policewoman in the corner stood up, gave a nervous smile. Rebecca caught a glance at herself in the full-length mirror: swollen, disheveled. Alan paced the room.

—I'd like to be alone with my wife.

Rebecca lifted her head. *Wife:* it was like a word that might remain on a page, though the page itself was plunged into darkness.

Alan repositioned the wicker chair and let out a long sigh. It was plain to see that he was seeking the brief adulation of grief. He needed the loss to attach itself to him. Why hadn't she woken? he asked. Was the door to her bedroom open or closed?

Had she slept through her alarm? Had Tomas eaten any breakfast? How far could he swim? Why didn't you get him a wetsuit that fit? Why didn't you hide it away? Did you give him his limits? You know he needs his limits.

She thought about that ancient life in the Dublin hills, the shiny kitchen, the white machinery, the German cars in the pebbled driveway, the clipped bushes, the alarm system, the security cameras, the *limits*, yes, and how far the word might possibly stretch before it rebounded.

—Did he have gloves on?

—Oh, stop, please, Alan.

—I need to know.

The red lights of the clock shone. It had been twelve hours. She lay on the bed.

—No, he had no gloves on, Alan.

She could not shake the Israeli story from her head. An Arab couple had lost their children to two illnesses over the course of five years: one to pneumonia, the other to a rare blood disorder. It was a simple story—small, intimate, intense. The father worked as a crane driver in the docklands of Haifa, the mother as a secretary in a corrugated-paper firm. Their ordinary lives had been turned inside out. After the children died, the father filled a shipping container with their possessions and every day moved it, using the giant crane and the skyhooks, to a new site in the yard, carefully positioning it alongside the sea: shiny, yellow, locked.

—He feels invincible, doesn't he?

—Oh, Jesus, Alan.

The search parties were spread out along the cliffs, their hopeless whistles in the air, her son's name blown back by the wind. Rebecca pushed open the rear sliding doors to the balcony. The sky was shot through with red. A stray sycamore branch touched her hair. She reached up. A crushing pain split her shoulder blade: her rotator cuff.

Cigarette smoke lingered in the air. She rounded the back of the cottage. A woman. Plainclothes. The whistles still came in short, sharp bursts.

A loss had lodged itself inside her. Rebecca gestured for the cigarette, drew long and hard on the filter. It tasted foul, heavy. She had not smoked in many years.

—He's deaf, you know, she said, blowing the smoke sideways.

A tenderness shone in the detective's eyes. Rebecca turned back into the house, pulled on her coat, walked out the front door and down toward the cliffs.

A helicopter broke the dark horizon, hovered for a moment right above the cottage, its spotlight shining on the stone walls, until it banked sharply and continued up the coast.

She joined the searchers. They went in groups of three, linking arms. The land was potholed, hillocked, stony. Every now and then she could hear a gasp from a neighboring group when a foot rolled across a rock, or a lost lobster pot, or a piece of rubbish. The stone walls were cold to the touch. The wind ripped under a sheet of discarded plastic. Tiny tufts of dyed sheep wool shone on the barbed wire: patterns of red and blue.

Along the coast small groups zigzagged the distant beaches in the last of the light. Dozens of boats plied the waves. The bells on the ancient boats tinkled. A Galway hooker went by with its white sails unfurled. A fleet of kayaks glided close to the shore, returning home.

The moon rose red: its beauty appeared raw and offensive to her. She turned inland. Two detectives walked alongside. Rebecca felt suspended between them. Cones of pale torch beam swept through the gathering darkness.

At an abandoned home, roofless, hemmed in by an immense rhododendron bush, a call came over the radio that a wetsuit had been found, over. The male detective held a finger in the air, as if figuring the direction of the wind. No, not a wetsuit, said the voice, high alert, no, there was something moving, high alert, stand by, stand by, there was something alive, a ripple in the water, high alert, high alert, yes, it was a body, a body, they had found something, over, a body, over.

The detective turned away from her, moved into the overgrown doorway, shielded the radio, stood perfectly still in the starlight until the call clarified itself: it was a movement in the water, discard, they had seen a seal, discard the last report, only a seal, repeat, discard, over.

Rebecca knew well the legend of the selkie. She thought of Tomas zippering his way out into the water, sleek, dark, hidden.

The female detective whispered into the radio: For fucksake, be careful, we've got the mother here.

The word lay on her tongue now: *mother, máthair, em.* They went forward again, through the unbent grass, into the tunnels of their torches.

ALAN'S CLOTHING WAS FOLDED on the wicker chair. His knees were curled to his chest. A shallow wheeze came from the white of his throat. A note lay on her pillow: *They wouldn't let me sleep in Tomas's room, wake me when you're home.* And then a scribbled *Please.*

They had called off the search until morning but she could hear the fishing boats along the coast, still blasting their horns.

Rebecca took off her shoes, set them by the bedroom fire. Only a few small embers remained, a weak red glow. The cuffs of her jeans were wet and heavy from the muck. She did not remove them.

She went to the bed and lay on top of the covers, pulled up a horsehair blanket, turned away from Alan. Gazing out the window, she waited for a bar of light to rise and part the dark. A torchlight bore past in a pale shroud. Perhaps there was news. At the cliff he had twirled the imaginary cane. Where had he learned that Chaplin shuffle? The sheer surprise of it. The unknowability. Unspooling himself along the cliff.

From the living room came the intermittent static of the radios. Almost eighteen hours now.

Rebecca pushed her face deeper into the pillow. Alan stirred underneath the sheets. His arm came across her shoulder. She lay quite still. Was he sleeping or awake? How could he sleep? His arm tightened around her. His hand moved to her hair, his fingers at her neck, his thumb at the edge of her clavicle.

That was not sleep. That was not sleep at all.

She gently pushed his arm away.

Another torch bobbed past the window. Rebecca rose from the bed. A gold-backed hairbrush lay on the dressing table. Long strands of her dark hair were tangled up inside it. She brushed only one side of her hair. The damp hem of her jeans chilled her toes and she walked toward the wicker chair, covered herself in a blanket, looked out into the early dark.

When dawn broke, she saw the door open slightly, the female detective peeping in around the frame, something warm in the eye-flicker between them.

Alan stirred, pale in the bed, and moaned something like an excuse. His pinkish face. His thinning hair. He looked brittle to her, likely to dissolve.

In the kitchen the kettle was already whistling. A row of tea-cups were set along the counter. The detective stepped forward and touched her arm. Rebecca's eyes leaped to catch hers, a brief merged moment.

—I hope you don't mind. We took the liberty. There's no news yet.

The presence of the word *yet* jolted her. There would, one day, be news. Its arrival was inevitable.

—We took one of Tomas's shirts from the wash basket.

—Why? said Rebecca.

—For the dogs, the detective said.

Rebecca wanted suddenly to hold the shirt, inhale its odor. She reached for the kettle, tried to pour through the shake in her hands. So, there would be dogs out on the headland later. Searching for her son. She glanced at her reflection in the window, saw only him. His face was double-framed now, triple-framed. Out on the headland, running, the dogs following, a ram, a hawk, a heron. She felt a lightness swell in her. A curve in the air. A dive. She gripped the hem of the counter. The slow, sleek slip of the sea. A darkening underwater. The shroud of cold. The coroner, the funeral home, the wreaths, the plot, the burial. She felt herself falter. The burst to the surface. A selkie, spluttering for air. She was guided into a chair at the table. She tried to lean forward to pour the tea. Voices vibrated around her. Her hands shook. Every outcome was unwhisperable. She had a sudden thought that there was no sugar in the house. They needed sugar for their tea. She would go to the store with Tomas later. The newsagent's. Yes, that is where she would go. Inland along the bend of narrow road. Beyond the white bungalow. Crossing at the one traffic light. Walk with him past the butcher shop, past the sign for tours to the islands, past the turf accountant, past the shuttered hotel, the silver-kegged alleyway, into the newsagent's on Main Street. The clink of the anchor-shaped bell. The black-and-white linoleum floor. Along the aisle. The sharp smell of paraffin. Past the paper rack set up on lobster pots, the small blue-and-orange ropes hanging down, old relics of the sea. She would walk beyond the news of his disappearance. Bread, biscuits, soup. To the shelf where the yellow packets of sugar lay. We cannot do without sugar, Tomas, second shelf down, trust me, there, good lad, get it, please, go on, reach in.

She wasn't sure if she had said this aloud or not, but when she looked up again the female detective had brought one of Tomas's shirts, held it out, her eyes moist. The buttons were cold to the touch: Rebecca pressed them to her cheek.

From the laneway came the sound of scraping branches. Van doors being opened and closed. She heard a high yelp, and then the scrabble of paws upon gravel.

SHE SPENT THAT MORNING out in the fields. Columns of sunlight filtered down over the sea. A light wind rippled the grass at the cliff edge. She wore Tomas's shirt under her own, tight and warm.

So many searchers along the beaches. Teachers. Farmers. Schoolchildren holding hands. The boats trawling the waters had trebled.

At lunchtime, dazed with fatigue, Rebecca was brought home. A new quiet had insinuated itself into the cottage. The policemen came and went as if they had learned from long practice. They seemed to ghost into one another. It was almost as if they could slip into one another's faces. She knew them, somehow, by the way they drank their tea. Food had arrived, with notes from neighbors. Fruit bowls. Lasagna. Tea bags and biscuits. A basket of balloons, of all things. A scribbled prayer to Saint Christopher in a child's hand.

Alan sat down next to her on the couch. He put his hand across hers. He would, he said, do the media interviews. She would not have to worry about it.

She heard the thud of distant waves. The labored drone of a TV truck filtered down from the laneway.

A Sunday newspaper called, offering money for a photograph. Alan walked to a corner of the cottage, cupped his phone, whispered into the receiver. She thought she heard him weeping.

Pages from the Israeli novel were strewn across her desk. Scribbles in the margins. Beside the pages, Mandelstam's memoir lay open, a quarter of the way through. Russia, she thought. She would have to tell them in Vladivostok, let them know what had happened, fill out the paperwork. The orphanage. The broken steps. The high windows. The ocher walls. The one great painting in the hallway: the Bay of Amur, summertime, a yacht on its water, water, always water. She would find the mother and father, explain that their son had disappeared swimming on the western seaboard of Ireland. A small apartment in the center of the city, a low coffee table, a full ashtray, the mother wan and withdrawn, the father portly and thuggish. My fault. I gave him a wetsuit. All my fault. Forgive me.

She wanted the day to peel itself backward, regain its early brightness, its possibility, its pour into teacups, but she was not surprised to see the dark come down.

Alan sat in the corner, curled around his phone. She almost felt a sadness for him, the whispered *sweetheart*, the urgent pleading and explanations with his own young children.

She totaled up the hours: forty-eight. That night, lying next to him, Rebecca allowed his arm across her waist. The simple comfort of it. She heard him murmur her name again, but she did not turn.

In the morning she rose and walked out behind the house, the dew wet against her plimsolls. The television truck hummed farther up the laneway, out of sight. She stepped across the cattle grid. The steel bars pushed hard into the soles of her feet. A muddy path led up the hill. The grass in the middle was green and untrodden. Moss lay slick on the stone wall.

A piece of torn plastic was tangled in the high hedges. She reached in and pulled it out, shoved it deep into her pocket: she had no idea why.

Water dripped from the branches of nearby trees. A few birds marked out their morning territory. She had only ever driven this part of the laneway before. It was, she knew, part of an old famine road.

Rebecca stood a while: the hum from the TV truck up the road seemed to cancel the rhythm of the sea.

She leaned into the hard slope of the road, opened the bar of the red gate, stepped over the mud. The bolt slid back perfectly into its groove. She walked the center grass up and around the second corner to where the TV truck idled against the hedges. Inside, silhouetted against a pair of sheer curtains, three figures were playing cards. The curtains moved but the figures remained static. Across the front seat a man lay slumped, sleeping.

A small group of teenagers huddled near the back of the truck, sharing a cigarette, their breath shaping clouds of white in the cold. They nudged each other as she approached.

She stopped, then, startled by the sight. Alone, casual, adrift. He sauntered in behind the group, unnoticed. A brown hunting jacket hung from his shoulders. A hooded sweatshirt underneath. His trousers were rolled up and folded over. The laces of his boots were open and the tongues wagged sideways. Steam rolled off him, as if he had been walking a long time.

His mouth was slightly open. His lip was wet with mucus. Mud and leaves in the fringes of his hair. Under his right arm he carried a dark bag. The bag fell from his arm, and he caught hold of it as he moved forward. A long, gray stripe. The wetsuit. He was carrying the wetsuit.

Sh'khol. He had not yet seen her. His body seemed to drag his shadow behind him: slow, reluctant, but sharp. She knew the word now. *Shadowed.*

The door of the TV truck opened behind her. Her name was called. Mrs. Barrington. She did not turn. She felt as if she were skidding in a car.

She was aware of a bustle behind her, two, three, four people piling out of the truck. The impossible utterance of his name. Tomas. Is that you? Turn this way, Tomas. A yell came from the teenagers. Look over here. They had their phones out. Tomas! Tomas! Turn this way, Tomas.

Rebecca saw a furred microphone pass before her eyes. It dipped down in front of her, and she pushed it away. A camera-man jostled her. Another shout erupted. She moved forward. Her feet slipped in the mud.

Tomas turned. She took him in her arms. A surge of joy.

She held his face. The paleness, the whites of his eyes. His was a gaze that belonged to someone else, a boy of another ex-perience.

He passed the wetsuit to her. It was cold to the touch and dry.

THE NEWS WENT AHEAD of them. The cheers went up as they rounded the corner toward the garden. Alan ran along the laneway in his pajamas, stopped abruptly when he saw the tele-vision cameras, grabbed for the gap in the cotton trousers.

Rebecca shouldered Tomas through the gauntlet, her arm encircling him tightly, guiding him to the front door.

In the cottage, a swathe of light dusted the floor. The female detective stood in the center of the room. Her name badge glinted. Detective Harnon. It struck Rebecca that she could name things again: people, words, ideas. A warmth spread through the small of her back.

A smell of turf smoke came off Tomas's clothing. It was, she later realized, one of the few clues she would ever get.

The cottage filled up behind her. She saw a photographer at the large plate-glass window. All around her the phones were ringing. The kettle whistled on the stove. A fear had tightened Tomas. She needed to get him alone. The photographer shoved his camera up against the windowpane. She spun Tomas away as the flash erupted.

Morning light stamped itself in small rectangles on the bedroom floor. Rebecca closed the window blinds. The helmet was lying on the bed. His pajamas were neatly folded and placed on a chair. She ignored the knocking at the door. He was shivering now. She held his face, kissed him. He looked away.

The door opened tentatively.

—Leave us be, please. Leave us be.

She touched the side of his cheek, then shucked the brown jacket from his shoulders. A hunting jacket. She checked the pockets. A few grains of thread. A small ball of fur. A wet matchbook. He lifted his arms. She peeled the sweatshirt up over his head. His skin was tight and dimpled.

A piece of leaf fell from his hair to the floor. She turned him around, looked at his back, his neck, his shoulder blades. He was unmarked. No cuts, no scrapes.

She looked down at Tomas's trousers. Denims. Too large by far. A man's denims. Fastened with an old purple belt with a gold clasp. Clothing from another era. Gaudy. Ancient.

A bolt of cold ran along her arms.

—No, she said. Please, no.

She reached for him, but he slapped her hand away. The door rattled again behind her. She turned to see Alan's face: the stretched wire of his flesh, the small brown of his eyes.

—We need a male detective in here, she said. Now.

IN THE HOSPITAL IT was still bright morning and the air was motionless in the low corridors and muddy footprints lay about and the yellow walls pressed in upon them and the pungent odor of antiseptic made her go to the windows and the trees outside stood static and the seagulls cawed up over the rooftops and she stood in the prospect of the unimaginable—the tangle of rumor and evidence and fact—and she waited for the doctors as the minutes idled and the nurses passed by in the corridors and the trolleys rattled and the orderlies pushed their heavy carts and an inexhaustible current of human misery moved in and out of the waiting room every story every nuance every pulse of the city pushing up against the wired windows peering in.

THE WATER POURED HARD and clear. She tested its warmth against her wrist. Tomas came into the bathroom, dropped his red jumper on the floor, slid out of his khakis, stood in his white shirt, clumsily working the buttons.

She reached to help, but he stepped away, then gestured for her to leave while he climbed into the swimming togs. So, he

wanted to wear shorts while she washed him? Fair enough, it
was appropriate, she would let him.

The house was quiet again. Only the sound of the waves. She
keyed her new phone alive. A dozen messages. She would attend
to them later.

She returned to the bathroom with her hands covering her
eyes.

—Ta-da! she said.

He stood there, pale and thin in front of her. The swimming
shorts were far too tight. Along his slender stomach she could
see a gathering of tiny, fine hairs that ran in a line from his belly
button. He hopped from foot to foot and cupped his hands over
the intimate outline of his body.

He had been untouched. That is what Detective Harnon had
said. He was slightly dehydrated, but untouched. No abuse. No
cuts. No scars. They had run all manner of tests. Later the detective had asked around the village. Nobody had come forward.
There were no other clues.

They wanted him to come in for evaluation the following
week. A psychologist, she said. Someone who might piece together everything that had happened, but Rebecca knew there'd
never be any answers, no amount of probing could solve it, no
photographs, no maps, no walks along the coastline. She would
go swimming with him again, soon, down to the water. They
would ease themselves into the shallows. She would watch him
carefully negotiate the seastack. She would guide him away

from the current. Perhaps some small insight might unravel, but she was aware that she could never finally, fully understand.

The simple grace of his return was enough. *I live, I breathe, I go, I come back.* Nothing else. *I am here now, that is all.*

Rebecca tested the water again with her fingers. She helped Tomas over the rim of the tub. Goose bumps appeared on his skin. His ribs were sharp and pale. He fell against her, stepped out. He groaned. The wet of his toes chilled her bare feet. She threw a towel around his shoulders to warm him, then guided him back toward the water. He placed both feet in the bath, and let the warmth course up through his body. He cupped his hands in front of his shorts once more. She put her hand on his shoulder and, with gentle insistence, got him to kneel.

He slid forward into the water.

—There we go, she said in Hebrew. Let me wash that mop.

She perched at the edge of the bath, took hold of his shoulder blades, ran a pumice stone over his back, massaged the shampoo into his hair. His skin was so very transparent. The air in his lungs changed the shape of his back. She applied a little conditioner to his scalp. His hair was thick and long. She would have to get it cut soon.

Tomas grunted and leaned forward, tugged at the front of his bathing shorts. His shoulders tautened against her fingers. She knew, then, what it was. He bent over to try to disguise himself against the fabric of the shorts. Rebecca stood without looking at him, handed him the soap and the sponge.

Impossible to be a child forever. A mother, always.

—You're on your own now, she said.

She moved away, closed the door and stood outside in the corridor, listening to his stark breathing and the persistent splash of water, its rhythm sounding out against the faint percussion of the sea.

TREATY

1

She is falling, ever so faintly, into age. It is not the slowness of rising in the morning, or the weariness of eyesight, or the chest pains that appear with more and more regularity, but the brittleness of memory that disturbs her now—how the past can glide away so easily, how the present can drift, how they sometimes collide—so that when she sees her torturer on television, she is not sure if her imagination is playing tricks, or if he has simply sifted through the sandbox of memory, slid headlong down the channel of thirty-seven years to tease her into a terrible mistake, or if it is truly him, appearing now on the late Spanish-language news, casual, handsome, controlled.

A crisp blue shirt with an open neck. His teeth white against the dark of his skin. A poised offhandedness to the manner in which he holds himself, at a conference, with several others, a row of microphones set up in front of them.

His appearance is so sudden at the tail end of the news that she pulls back sharply in her armchair, startling the two other Sisters on the couch.

Beverly holds her hand in the air to reassure them: *All right, sorry, only me, go back to sleep.*

She leans to turn up the volume on the remote but his image is gone, the report tailing off, a young blonde reporter staring confidently into the camera. A shot from along the river Thames. How is that possible? Perhaps she has garbled the images, confused the reports? The geography alone is too dizzying to contemplate.

The slippages of memory have happened so much recently. Mangled sentences, mislaid keys, forgotten names. Rainshowers of words, then drought. Only last week, she got lost on a walk along the beach in the bay, took the wrong path out of the dunes, the wind whipping the grass around her feet. Three miles from the house, she had to ask someone to phone a cab. Even then she couldn't remember the exact address.

Too many uncertainties, so that even the absolute certainties— the day of the week, the tie of a shoelace, the rhythm of a prayer— have been called into question. And yet there's something about the man's face—if only for a split second—that sluices a sense of ice along the tunnel of her spine. The one brief close-up. The way he held himself on the screen, amidst a line of dignitaries. What was it exactly? The peculiar poise that age had brought upon him? The access to the microphones? The flagrant manner of his reappearance? The single quick close-up?

Her torturer. Her abuser. Her rapist.

IN THE HALF-MOONLIGHT AT the back of the house, Beverly reaches into her cardigan pocket for her lighter.

She is the only smoker amongst the Sisters. An ancient habit from her childhood in Ireland, she has carried it with her all these years: Belgium, Marseilles, Colombia, Saint Louis, Baltimore, the girls' home in Houston, and now the southern shore of Long Island.

A quiet getaway, she was told. A retreat for a month or two. Fresh sea air. A time for repose. But she had felt the doom of it all: seventy-six years old, arriving with a single suitcase to a place of final worship.

She taps a cigarette, rolls the flint on the lighter, inhales deeply. The smoke is dizzying. Already the tin coffee can is a quarter full of ash and butts. Her fellow Sisters have grown to tolerate her weakness, even grudgingly admire it, the tall, thin Irish nun with her maverick routine of aloneness.

She watches the cold and the smoke together shape the air. Behind her, the lights in the house flicker off, one by one, the other Sisters off to their prayers.

The trees stand stark against the sky. It is fall, or autumn: sometimes she loses track of which word belongs where. Small matter, it is that time of year when the dark descends early.

She smokes her second cigarette and scrunches it out in the grass at her feet, leans down, searches among the cold blades for the filter, drops it in the hanging coffee can.

That was him. It was most certainly him.

A gust of wind shuts the screen door sharply behind her. She reaches out her arms like someone recently blind. The darkness more visible as her eyes adjust.

In the living room she pauses at the large digital television. A row of lights shine from the contraptions underneath: a cable box, a DVD player. She slips her hand along the edge of the television but can find no buttons. She fumbles in the dark for the remote, bumps against the side of the coffee table. A musty smell rises from the carpet. A dropped spoon. A fallen newspaper.

Only then does she think to strike her lighter.

In the bright flare she spies the head of the remote slipped down between the sofa cushions. A row of menu items, HDM1, HDM2, PC. One needs to be a nuclear engineer these days just to bring a machine to life. She clicks through. Vampires. Baseball. Cop shows. She is tempted, for a moment, to remain with the Mormon wives.

There are three Spanish-language channels all in close proximity to one another. Surely, at some stage during the night, there will be a repeat. She pulls a cushion tight against her stomach. The digital clock flickers. There is, she knows, a way to record the show, even to freeze the screen—one of the Sisters did it last week during a CBS special on the Shroud—but she might lose the image altogether.

When the report finally comes on, she slides off the couch, onto the floor, sits close to the television. London. A series of peace talks. Representatives from all sides gathering together. An array of microphones set up on a table. A line of five men, two women.

The hairs along her arm bristle: Please, Lord, let it not be him.

The words tangle and braid. *Guerilla, peace accord, land rights, low-level talks, reconciliation, treaty.*

Then it is him. For three short seconds. She reaches her hand toward his face, recoils. His heavy-lidded eyes. His pixelated mouth. He is close-shaven, sharp, his hair neatly cut. He is a little heavier, more compact. He does not speak, but there is no mistake. He has taken on the aura of a diplomat.

She sits back against the couch, fumbles for her cigarettes. Make Yourself present, Lord. Come to my aid.

When he slapped her face, he would call her *puta*. In the jungle cage he pulled back her hair, yanked it so hard that her neck felt as if it would snap. A whisper. In her ear. As if he himself couldn't afford to hear the words. *Pendeja*. In the safe house where she was taken for four weeks, in the white room where she watched the caterpillars crawl along the cracks in the walls, he would read to her aloud from the newspaper before he yanked open her blouse and bit her breast until it bled.

SHE IS WOKEN IN the early morning by Sister Anne who sits quietly at the side of the bed. The curtains have been slightly parted.

She pulls back the bed covers, swings her legs out, fumbles for her slippers. She can tell by the angle of light that she has missed morning prayer.

—I overslept. I'm so sorry.

—There's something we must talk about, Beverly.

—Of course.

Sister Anne is a woman who has aged gracefully apart from a shallow set of accordion lines that seem to hurry toward her cheekbones, giving her a vaguely scattershot look.

—By the television, she says. Last night.

It takes Beverly a moment for the evening to return, as if from one of those ancient sets she knew as a child in Galway, a quick flare of light and then a slow bromiding outward. The recollection of his face. The chill that ripped along her body. The manner in which he was constructed, square upon digital square, all the new edges to him.

—I think I must have woken from, I might, I may have been dreaming.

—Well, it's unfortunate, but I'm afraid I'm going to have to ask you to stop.

—Of course.

She is unsure of what it is that she must stop. The house is meant as a retreat. None of the Sisters have been told of her background, only that she lived in South America once, that she has come from Houston, that she is suffering exhaustion, she is here to rediscover sleep, that is all.

What she needs now is to get beyond the first bruised moments of waking. To make her bed, to take a shower, to say her dailies.

Sister Anne rises from the chair and only then does Beverly notice that she has brought her a cup of coffee and a biscuit on a saucer. The small mercies.

—Thank you.

Sister Anne turns at the door, haloed in fluorescence from the hallway, and says gently: There will be no need to pay for it, of course.

—Pay for it?

—There are, Beverly, two cigarette burns in the carpet.

AT THE HOME IN HOUSTON the girls had been surprised to find a nun they could smoke with. They thought her so tall. Sister Stretch. The home was set up next to a clinic. Theirs was an open-door policy. The girls came and went. The corridors hummed. Mornings in the kitchen, afternoons in the counseling room, evenings out combing streets of half-lamplight: Hermann Park, Montrose, Sunnyside, Hiram Clarke, the Fifth Ward. Whole nights spent awake in the convent house. The protests outside. The shouting. The placards. The bullhorns. She and her Sisters were condemned from the pulpit. Radicals, dissenters. They never thought themselves anything of the sort. It was simply a home, a place for the girls to stay. She counseled them. Children with children. She made no political stance. *Abortion, pro-life, anti-woman.* The words did not concern her. The language seemed designed to only merchandise flesh. She wanted to be mute in everything but action. To give a shoulder. To take an elbow. To feel her feet strike the ground. She worked late into the night. She listened in church to the priest railing against her, his voice high and indignant. She bowed her head. She accepted the invective. She still took the sacrament. On principle, she never escorted the girls to the clinic, but she watched them go and collected them afterward, took their arms, walked them through the gauntlet. Sometimes the same girls returned, just months later, bearing children once more. Exhaustion got her. Three times she collapsed in the community room. They found her eventually in the chapel, slumped over, a trickle of blood from her nose. She was shocked when, in the downtown hospital, a nurse showed her a mirror: the darkness beneath her eyes looked tattooed in. The emergency-room doctors had mistaken her, at first, as homeless. They ripped off her clothes. She struggled to pull the sheet back across. What perplexed them were the scars on her breasts, how she hid them, the hard jagged lines, their peculiar tracery.

THE WIND RIPPLES THE dune grass. She wears a long blue skirt, a dark cardigan, an orange windbreaker. Lay clothes, always. She has not, for forty years, worn any formal clothing, just the simple wooden cross beneath her blouse.

A clean, plain silence rolls along the shore, made cleaner and plainer still by the occasional screech of gulls. It seems to her that some vast hand lies behind the dunes flinging the birds in patterns out over the Atlantic. Far out on the horizon, a tanker disappears from view, as if dropping off the edge of the sea.

Beverly has crumpled her last cigarettes in the cardigan pocket. She likes the feel of the grains, the fall of them from her fingers, sprinkling them now in the cold sand. She cannot remember a time, even in captivity in the jungle, when she went without cigarettes. She places a few grains of tobacco upon her tongue. Raw. Bitter. They will be of no comfort. What was it about his appearance that had corralled her so easily? Why had she stayed up so late with the other Sisters? Why had she watched the Spanish-language news? The odd little magpie of the mind. Nothing is finally finished, then? The past emerges and re-emerges. It builds its random nest in the oddest places.

She struggled for so many years with absolution, the depth of her vows, poverty, chastity, obedience. Working with doctors, experts, theologians to unravel what had happened. Every day she went to the chapel to beseech and pray. Hundreds of hours trying to get to the core of it, understand it, pick it apart. Forgiveness for herself first, they told her. In order, then, to forgive him. Without hubris, without false charity. Therapy sessions, physical exams, spiritual direction, prayer. The embrace of Christ's agony. The abandonment at the hour. Opening herself to compassion. Trying to put it behind her with the mercy of time. The days slipping by. Small rooms. Long hours. The curtains opening and closing. The disappearance of light. The blackened mirrors. The days spent weeping. The guilt. She sheared her hair. Swept the rosary beads off the bedside table. Took baths fully clothed. No burning bush, no pillar of light. More a pail of acid into which she wanted to dissolve. And here he is, back now, once more. Or perhaps she has simply dreamt it? One of those momentary aftershocks, rippling under the surface? A small pulse of the wound where there used to be a throb?

They had told her, years ago, that it might happen. In Saint Louis, in the convent hospital, along the dark waters of the Mississippi. The anger. The shame. The false pride. The disgrace. It would return. She built up a wall of prayer. *Neither life nor death, nothing can separate me from Your love and mercy. If I pass through raging waters in the sea, Lord, I shall not drown.* She repeated the prayers over and over. Stone upon stone. A finished wall. Yet why is it now that she has allowed him to scale it? He is, after all, only a man on television, the image of an image. But so well dressed. So poised. So public. What right does he have to talk about peace? What had he done to achieve such grace?

Back along the roadway, she passes a deckchair left over from the summer, its innards fluttering in the wind. The sand blows in swirled patterns on the footpath. She pulls the padded hood up around her face, reaches up and presses the bridge of her nose between her fingers.

A two-mile walk back to the convent house. She has, at least, a sturdy pair of shoes.

Flip-flops. Made from car tires. Slapping against the soles of her feet. She was dragged from the jeep. Blindfolded, driven away. Rushed down a mud road. A clearing in the bamboo. On the first night her feet swelled with insect bites. By the second night, they had bled and festered. Eventually they gave her rubber boots for the marches. Always on the move. From one clearing in the jungle to the next. They thought her first a human-rights worker. She wore lay clothes. She worked alone. Word filtered out on the radio: she was a Maryknoll, a nun. He didn't believe it. He ripped the wooden cross from her neck. She said nothing. Other nuns had been shot. She was nothing special. He spat when she prayed. He was so young then. No more than twenty-three, twenty-four. Already a commander and the hatred had hardened in him, but she thought for sure that she could find some point of tenderness. She used to imagine dropping her words behind his eyes to find a soft point, in his memory, some prayer, some word, something maternal she could jolt from him. He knew none of the rhythms of prayers: he had grown up without them. No nursery rhymes. Only the right-wing paramilitary songs, none of which she knew. She would somehow reach him, she was sure of it—but he remained aloof, absent. Even when there were others alongside her in captivity, aid workers, radicals, professors, and once, for a few days, a left-wing senatorial candidate. Five months in the jungle, four weeks in a safe house—six months in all. His ability to stare. That thousand-yard remove. He had a mole on his cheek. Was it still there? Last night she had reached out and touched the ghost of his face, the television static. Surely she would have noted the absence of the mole. Why had she not thought of it before? Why hadn't she recorded the program? She could have destroyed it, rid herself of him. What have I done? Forgive me, Lord.

Once he took off his bandana and stuffed it in her mouth to stop her from making noise, so that toward the end she just lay there, compliant, a vague freedom in the shame, the thought of elsewhere, the west of Ireland, the stone walls, the rain permanent across the fields, her mother's face, flushed with disgrace, the shape of her father moving out into the laneway, her brother

walking down the road, away from her, that childhood, gone, a
bead of his sweat dripping down on the bridge of her nose, *puta*,
he pushed her head down against the dirt, *puta*, the sound of his
voice, quiet and controlled, *puta*.

She is startled by the toot of a horn behind her and the hiss of
car tires. It has begun to gently drizzle.

—Coming home?

As if in synch, Sister Anne and Sister Yun lean toward her,
earnest, expectant. Such an odd word, *home*. She finds herself
trying to speak, but the words are lodged inside her somehow,
not so much in her throat but in the hollow of her stomach, and
when she responds she is startled by the rise of the sounds
through her: *Sí, gracias, a casa, es un poco frío,* so incongruent
and displaced, she has no idea how she has lapsed so easily into
Spanish, how she has allowed him so immediately back into her
life, when she was sure that he had died, or faded into the jungle
again, or disappeared.

Carlos had escaped. Rumors of death squads, retribution.
She kept up on the news in sporadic bursts, but she never allowed it to slip under her skin, not since Saint Louis anyway.
After that, a shelter in Baltimore, then the girls' home in Houston. Deeper wounds, other lives. The life of a Maryknoll. There
were some over the years who had tried to make of her a hero-
ine, a figurehead, a political autograph, and she knew that they
whispered behind her back, of book deals, movie contracts.
Even her brother in England had wanted to make a radio documentary, but she preferred to think of other things, life in the

village before she was captured, the volume of blue sky, the children in the schoolhouse, the fall of rain on the tin roof, the dust rising from the dirt floor of her shack, the yellow barrel at the back of the classroom, the wooden ladle dipping for rainwater, the stick of chalk in her cigarette box, the faulty carburetor in the jeep, she was always trying to fix it, she leaned across the engine, the chalk dissolving in the rain.

—Hurry up now, Beverly.

She slips her hands from the pockets of her cardigan, slides into the backseat. The window powers up.

—You'll catch your death.

On the front dashboard Sister Yun performs a little drumroll with long thin fingers.

—We must not miss the three o'clock.

The Hour of Great Mercy, the most fervent of her prayers, the time of Christ's dying on the cross. In the jungle she would listen for a guard's radio, and it grew so that she could almost tell the time by the angle of sun through the trees.

—Are you sure you're all right, Beverly?

—You're hardly wrapped up at all.

—You must be freezing.

She watches as Sister Anne adjusts the rearview mirror.

—What's that you were saying?

Sister Anne's rosary beads click against the steering wheel as she guides the car into the road.

—Oh, nothing really. My mind wanders sometimes. Forgive me. *Frío.* I think I said it's cold.

The two elderly nuns lock eyes in the mirror a moment. She glances away, grateful for the silence, until Sister Anne reaches forward to put NPR on the radio: a drone attack in Afghanistan, a typhoon in the Philippines, a wildfire in Australia.

The car slides through the quiet Long Island town, the small boutiques, the coffee shops, the travel agency, the flower arrangement store, the *pastelería*.

THE HOUSE IS a recent gift to the Church. It has not yet been fully renovated, or consecrated, so it is still a place of mirrors. She sees herself everywhere. One in the front hallway, gilded and ornate, catching the reflection of the front steps, so that, at the doorway, one seems to be coming and going at the same time. A mirror, too, at the top of the winding stairs, near the Sacred Heart, with a fresh vase of flowers beneath it. A series of oil paintings along the corridor, with glass frames, so that at the wrong angle she can catch sight of herself as she moves along. In her bathroom there is another mirror which runs the length of the wall.

She thought first of obscuring it entirely, draping it with a cloth, but did not want to be rude, it was simply best to ignore, let it be.

Beverly stands pale, white, naked, scarred. She turns quickly from the mirror, steps into the shower, pulls the sliding door across. The water pumps cold at first and then the heat deepens. A strong pulse of water at her stomach, her shoulders, her neck. She applies the conditioner, rinses, holds, stands back once more, soaps her feet, her toes. Puts her head against the fresh cool tile of the wall. Feels the last drips fall down upon her back.

She steps out on the cold floor, turbans a towel around her head. After he bit her breast, he stitched it crudely himself, pulled the flap of it together and shoved a heated needle into it, pulled the medicated thread through. Wrapped up a bottle of antiseptic, ribboned it, gave it to her like a gift. When it became infected, he took her to the camp infirmary where they ripped her breast open again. He didn't go near her for weeks afterward. Twice she cut it open herself just to keep him at bay.

WITH HER BACK TO THE MIRROR, she towels herself off and dresses. The late news. The last moments of the day. The world at its least consoling. The dark falling outside. Everything moving toward sleep, or its lack. The elderly Argentinian sisters half-doze on the couch together. A copy of *Clarín* spread out in front of them. Trays and teacups. Magazines. The carpet has not been fixed, but the armchairs have been scooted forward to cover the cigarette burns. How was it that she didn't even notice? Not just once but twice. So reckless. She could have burned the whole place down. She cannot even remember lighting up.

A pulse of need whips through her. They say it is the most addictive drug of all. She will go tomorrow to the local pharmacy. Nicotine patches. Chewing gum. A matter of willpower.

She likes it here with her elderly Sisters, the informality, the openness, the sense that so much of their work has been done, that now it is time to sit back and watch time unfold, to pray in the face of the sorrows to which the world is still bound.

She watches the Sisters stir, both of them sitting up as if roped to one another.

—Can we watch the . . . a ver las noticias?

—Sí, sí, por que, no?

A report on the disappearance of the jaguar species in the Amazon. A mine collapse near Valparaiso. News of the elections in Guatemala. Toward the end of the news there is a small report of the London conference—minimal progress in the talks, something about narco-traffic, mining rights, a timeline for further peace talks in Havana—but there is no sight or mention of Carlos.

She should check the Internet, but for all these years she has managed to avoid it, leave it in the background, she is not even sure how to use it: the prospect is mildly terrifying.

—Demasiada tristeza, says Sister María, rising from her chair.

—Buenas noches.

Beverly watches as the two elderly women climb the stairs, shadow to shadow, their cardigans twined.

She waits all the way through the second repeat of the program, just in case. Ridiculous. As if the repeat might change itself and he might somehow appear, changed once again.

Has he become a man of peace somehow? Has he offered his cheek, Lord? Has he turned himself around? How many other things run counter to the life he once had? Who is he now? An elegant man in a blue shirt? A participant at a peace institute? What accident of circumstance brought the conference to London? How did he manage to shuck his past?

Only once she saw him almost crack. At the safe house near Puerto Boyacá. The windows were sealed and blackened. Whatever light came in crept under the door. Vague sounds from outside the door. A distant radio. She tried to remember old poems, prayers, psalms, even the way the words looked on the page. He unchained her and brought her a glass of coconut milk. She had no idea why. He came across the hard dirt floor. A slight limp. He wore black laced boots, his camouflage trousers tucked into them. A sheathed knife dangled from his belt. He kneeled down in front of her. His eyes heavy-lidded and brown. His cheeks unshaven. The flashlight stung her momentarily. She drew away. Carlos put one hand on the back of her neck and tilted her chin with his forefinger and had her drink: the milk was cool, though there was no fridge in the house. She could feel the coolness, a whole childhood of it, falling through her. Rain on the coral beach in Galway. White tennis balls on the broken court. Her brother at his shortwave radio. A nest of wires and voices. Her father's cattle huddled on a laneway. The broken church bell. A grass verge of green in the laneway. High windows. Too tall for the school chairs. The milk came in small silver cans. She would not cry or whimper. She had always refused him that. Carlos sat back against the wall and looked at her, his own lip quivering. She thought the milk to be the harbinger of some abuse—a punch to the ear, the knife to the throat, a heave against the wall—but he simply fed it to her, then drank from the same glass, muttered something that sounded like an apology, and left, closed the thick steel door behind him. A little rim of light leaked under the door.

IT IS TWO IN the morning by the clock on the DVD when she rises for bed. She shuffles across the kitchen floor, reaches to switch off the outdoor porch light. The ashtray still hangs there, the tin can moving ever so slightly in the breeze.

Beverly opens the screen door. The ashtray has not been emptied. She tilts it. The odor is foul.

She walks the length of the porch in the hard cold. The stars out, nailheading the night. A few clouds drifting. The trees shaped against the dark. She squeezes her thumbs against her forehead once more: To abase the self in such a way, no, I cannot. I must resist.

An alarming silence. There was a while in Saint Louis, years ago, when she simply could not stand to be outside: the very sound of insects drilled into her.

She reaches deftly into the bucket, smooths the crush from a misshapen cigarette, lights up.

On the lawn, a sudden square of light falls from an upstairs window, like the frame of a painting thrown onto the ground. She finishes the cigarette in three hard draws.

A swell of revulsion stabs her stomach and she sways, dizzy with regret.

Inside, she locks the door, puts her head against the frame. Is this what awaits me, Lord? Is this where I finish? Is this where You have led me?

There is a flick of shadow at the top of the stairs. A creak. Flecks of light ordering and reordering themselves. She moves through the darkened living room, grabs ahold of the banisters.

Sister Anne is sitting in the middle of the stairs in her dressing gown and slippers. No disapproval in the broad pale expanse of her forehead. No tightening of the lips. No shake of her head.

—Can't sleep?

—I'm just fidgety.

Beverly is well aware of the pungency of the cigarette. She pulls her breath in, turns to the wall, squeezes herself past the staircase mirror. Her face is lean and spectral, her neck striated.

—You know, Beverly, that I am here at any stage, if you need to talk.

—Of course.

—We are, in large measure, the prayers we share.

She turns quickly from her reflection, pauses at the top of the stairs in the red light from the Sacred Heart.

—Actually, I was thinking of making a little journey.

—Sorry?

—London. I was thinking of making a little journey to London.

A surge of panic: it is an idea so sudden and unplanned that she feels as if she has been sideswiped by her own shadow.

—Why ever so?

A cellar, an airless place, a mineshaft, a caterpillar crawl, a chain across the floor, a single bead of light underneath the door.

—I have a brother there.

—But you only just got here. Didn't the doctors say that you need to rest?

To bend, to shape, to break the truth. Have I become the liar I never wanted to become? Why not tell Sister Anne that she has just, quite simply, been knocked off balance? That she has seen a man she knew long ago? That he has resurfaced? That she must affirm it is him? That he is representing himself as a man of peace? That he is there in London now? That she must leave? That this is all she now knows, all she can tell?

—Is anything the matter with him?

—Sorry?

—Is something the matter with your brother?

—He's ill.

To survive one mistake she has committed herself to the next and then the next. She shifts her foot slightly on the stair.

As a child, her brother spent a year in bed with spinal tuberculosis. His room was full of crystals, coils, wires: he taught himself how to build model radios. He was six years younger than her, but she sat by his bed with him, listening to the chatter of ships from out on the Atlantic. Years later she wrote him letters, once a week, until he, too, left—first for Dublin, then Edinburgh, until he drifted down to London to review literature for the BBC. They fell into that life of distant brother and sister: the yearly Christmas cards, the occasional phone calls, the funerals of their parents. Drifting farther still until she was kidnapped. He had organized petitions for her then. Marches on the Dáil, the House of Commons, the Colombian embassy. Afterward he wanted to make the radio documentary about what had happened to her, but she couldn't do it. *They chained you? They beat you with a wooden board? They kept you locked up in a room? They fed you from a metal dish?* Paralyzed by the truth. He allowed her the silence. They fell into the old patterns again, talking once or twice a year, not so much out of neglect or embarrassment, but simply because that's how it seemed families worked, their seepage.

—He's ill, you say?

—Yes.

—Is he a smoker then too?

There is no malice in Sister Anne's question, but it stings her. So, you were watching me? You opened your curtains and the light fell on the lawn? You saw me reach into the coffee can? You smelled the smoke drifting up to your room? Have I become hostage yet again? Is this where I end up, after all these years? A room on Long Island, at the end of the continent, the water cresting silently against the shore?

—He'll be in my prayers.

—You're very kind.

—You'll have to get permission from your Order.

—They will pray alongside me, I'm sure.

—God measures us. He truly does.

—Yes, He does.

—Is there anything else you need to tell me, Beverly?

He put a chain around my neck. He ripped my breast. He violated me.

—No, she says, stepping through the guttering red light, along the landing. She pauses a moment at her door, leans against the frame, hears the click of Sister Anne's door.

The house falls quiet and the shadows fold down, dark.

2

Victoria Station. A crush of faces. A salmon-along of tourists. Her long skirt brushes the floor. Her suitcase has no wheels and the handle is unhinged so that she has to drag it behind her, reluctant, unwieldy. She would like a moment's respite. To sit down and take the weight off her legs. Find a refuge. A traveler's chapel maybe, or a small café with a quiet corner.

She is startled by a pigeon flapping along past a piano. The piano is, it seems, an art project, left in the train station for anyone to play.

The pigeon hovers, then lands a moment on the lid, walks along the beveled edge.

At a food stall Beverly buys herself a croissant and a cup of tea in a paper cup. Awful to drink tea from paper, the little tab of the teabag hanging down. There is nowhere to sit, so she drifts across to the piano, perches on the edge of the bench.

A pulsing pain in her lower back. The journey has been arduous, a two-hour delay in JFK, a runway incident in Heathrow, the wrong direction on the tube from Paddington—she was woken only when she got to the end of the line.

The pigeon returns and pecks at her feet. It is, she notices, extraordinarily fat, the color of a thing into which no color goes. How odd to think that it might live inside the station, a nest in the rafters, its whole life without a tree of any sort.

She lays her head against the lacquered edge of the piano and is shaken awake moments later by a pale young boy whose mother stands nearby, vaguely apologetic, wanting to play. For a moment she cannot recall where she is, or how she has gotten here.

—Don't forget your tea, Missus.

She pats the young boy on the head. A blessing upon him. Used to be, long ago, we could make the sign of the cross. Gone, those days. Maybe just as well: who knows what the mother might say if she attempted to bless the child?

Outside the light pours down hard and clear and yellow. The tea has grown tepid but she drains the last mouthful anyway. No rubbish can in sight. She crumples the cup and stuffs it in her cardigan pocket, moves toward the taxi line, nudging the suitcase along.

From a distance she is sure she hears the faint rumor of the piano: the boy is confident and agile beyond his years.

She nudges forward in the queue, pats her cardigan pocket, flicks through her passport, searching for her brother's address. A ticket stub, a few receipts, nothing else. Lord, help me now. I must find his address. Near Victoria Station. I remember that.

She lays the suitcase flat on the ground, thumbs open the steel lock. Three dresses, an overcoat, a change of shoes, a Thomas Merton book, a biography of the new Pope. An acute wave of helplessness sweeps over her, a nausea that begins in the pit of her stomach, rises and spreads.

—You all right there?

There is a tattoo at the collar of the taxi driver's shirt, the extension of a vine or a bramble of some sort. She flips the suitcase closed, snaps the locks, pushes down on the lid to keep herself from toppling forward, stands shakily.

He gazes up at her with mild alarm. She is a full head and shoulders taller than him. If she were to fall she might topple him.

—I lost the address. My brother. It was written down. It's . . . a cog in my head. It just comes and goes.

—Sorry, love, he says, can't help you there.

She watches as the driver opens his car door for another customer. A vine. Dark green. A line through the trees. The sound of a radio. A small steel lock on the door. Escape. It was easy enough to cut through the bamboo: once with a sharpened coat hanger, once with a piece of corrugated metal. She squeezed herself through the gap, crept along in her rubber-soled shoes. She got as far as the river, but it was so swollen with rain that it terrified her: she simply sank to her knees and waited, slumped against the trunk of a tree. They found her, covered head to toe in ant bites. When she recovered, she was beaten. He pulled a hood over her head. Darkness folded around her. The cloth smelled of rotting fruit. She vomited and he left her in the hood a few minutes, to stew. Afterward she mumbled her prayers. Rosary after rosary. Her body ached. She bled. It seeped through to her dress. Carlos allowed her to wash. The appalling embarrassment. Always turning away, hunched over, covering her breasts, her groin, bent into whatever shadow she might find. Someone watching from afar. She wondered what might happen if she ever conceived a child. One time, the clock of her body stopped for two months. It terrified her, then she bled again. She was not forsaken. She cleaned herself. *Immerse yourself in prayer wherever you happen to be.*

Beverly shuffles out from the taxi line and back under the awning of the railway station. The ambush of the mind. She has grown unreliable even to herself. These turnings, these slippages. The distant piano still sounds out. Perhaps that's the piped music of the station? What was the name of Ian's street? How did I get here? I had his address when I was at the airport. On the train. On the tube. Maybe it fluttered to the floor.

She wishes a moment to be back again with the girls in Houston. To conjure a safe place out of nothing. To return to the known, the benign, the easy. To stand with them at the back entrance. Sister Stretch. Perching on the back steps, smoking. Kneeling in the small basement chapel alongside her Sisters. Or even the simplicity of the convent house on Long Island. To walk along the beach and watch the gulls drawn through the dawn. Sister Anne. Sister Camille. The other Sister, the Argentinian, she cannot recall her name, what was it?

At the traffic light on Vauxhall Bridge Road, she pauses. It catches then, and she remembers: John Islip Street.

———

HE HAS GAINED A small paunch and his eyes are puffy as if sleep has eluded him for a while now, but he is still tall and elegant and silver-haired, the sort of man who insists on a tie even while alone in the late afternoon.

—Bev, he says.

Her childhood name. It reminds her of the stone bridge over the river in Oughterard, the water running quick and shallow and light-veined beneath her.

—What in the world are you doing here?

He reaches immediately for her suitcase. She stands a moment on the precipice of the apartment. The river ran swiftly west. Copper-colored in summertime. Fly-fishermen stood at the bend where the oak trees bowed. A low plain of red sky cupped over them.

He takes her arm and guides her toward the living room. An ancient coat of books on the walls: novels, photography collections, advance reading copies, poetry. Stacks of them piled every which way on the floor.

He sweeps five or six books from the lumpy brown couch. They skitter across the carpet to meet their fellows.

—Collision, she says.

Ian takes her hand. His fingers feel cold to the touch. What is it that he fills his days with now? What gives him pause? What, apart from books, jostles his mind? Even from a young age he never really believed in God, or ideas of poverty, purity, piety.

There were times, in recent years, on the phone, that he railed against the Catholic Church. The abuse. The scandals. The Magdalene Laundries. The deceitful morass of bureaucracy. The lives bought, he said, on the condition of the buyer's ignorance. She knew the flaws, the awful shame, the flagrant greed. She had no need to defend it, to protest. She, too, had doubted the Church—more deeply, perhaps, than her brother could ever have known. Not so much in the jungle, but afterward, in the crisp sheets of the Saint Louis hospital, where she admitted the terror, as if it had been set on delay. What was it that she herself had desired? What mirror had He thrust at her? There were days that the blame hit her with such force she could hardly stand. She told herself it was her fault: her body, her mind, her failure. She had enticed him. Asked for it. Deserved it. The days withheld their light. Her mind was an empty seed. The despair swelled in the husk of dark.

—Are you okay? What happened? Bev? You said collision.

—I did?

—I'll make tea. I'll get you a cup of tea.

—I'd like that, yes.

The rattle of teacups. He pokes his head around the corner.

—I'll be right there, he says, don't fall asleep.

She hears, then, the high whistle of the kettle and the soft sigh of the fridge door.

On one bookshelf stands a photograph of their parents sitting on the front bumper of an ancient motorcar, the large white headlights, the curved panels, the air horn. An impossible era. They stand remote from her, more photograph than memory.

Somewhere, deep in the apartment, she hears a voice, and then a burst of classical music. A radio piano.

Ian enters the room and carefully places the tray down on the table. Two china cups, a plate of biscuits, a teapot in a cozy. He is still a man of the ancient ways. He was married once, long ago, to a woman from Scotland, but they never had children. A woman of short hair and spectacles. A psycholinguist. They divorced. Ian had been afraid to tell Beverly at first. What was her name again? These words escaping, like slow punctured air from her lungs.

He pours the tea through a small metal strainer and holds the jug of milk up as if to measure not just her preference, but her demeanor.

—I think I might be forgetting things, Ian.

—Oh, God, no.

—It's not Alzheimer's, not that.

She pauses with the teacup at her mouth: Or, rather, not forgetting. I'm not sure what to say. It's a sort of remembering, I suppose.

—Whatever do you mean?

—He came back, you know.

—Who came back, Bev?

A curtain opens up on her brother's face, then, when she tells him: the exhaustion in Houston, the move to Long Island, the appearance on the television, the confusion, the doubt, the night on the stairs with Sister Anne, the constant return of Carlos's face as she walked along the beach, how he was a man of peace now, it rattled her, she could not shake it, she had to come see him, she had to see if perhaps it was true, is it possible to find peace when all along you have sought to destroy it, how is it that a man can change so entirely, where did the shift within him occur, what was the word she was looking for, *reconciliation?*

—And now he's at some peace conference?

—An institute, yes.

—And you want to see him?

—I don't even know for sure if it's him.

The quick flit of Ian's eyes: green, same as her own. A brother, then. Perhaps that is it? Perhaps Carlos had a brother? A cousin? She has never even entertained the notion. A twin even. The panic claws her throat. What if it's the simplest error of all and there is someone identical? An exact duplicate who is, in fact, the opposite?

Ian picks a biscuit from the plate, bites down softly, and lets it dissolve on his tongue.

—What day is it today?

—Sunday of course.

A sharp breath escapes her: Oh, I missed mass. The first time in my life. I missed mass, Ian. I can't believe I missed it.

—You've been traveling.

—I'm tired, Ian. So very, very tired.

She lifts the saucer toward the teacup to calm the shake in her hands.

—I'm sure there's some sort of dispensation, isn't there? Isn't there some sort of Catholic word?

He toes around in his books as if he might find the word in the mess on the floor.

—Indulgence, he says, snapping his fingers. Isn't that it? Indulgence?

SHE WAKES IN HIS BED: she has never once slept in a double bed before. An indulgence, yes. She stumbles, fully clothed, to the window, parts the blinds to the yellow streetlight. A sheen of wet on the ground. The light skids in patches along the footpath. She hears the laughter of two young women, tottering arm in arm down the street. A black taxi cab trawls slowly through the rain. Monday morning. A plenary indulgence.

In the corridor she hears the whirr of a computer printer. A light leaks out from a gap in the living-room door. Through the gap she sees Ian caught in a blue light, books scattered around him, bent into whatever work is at hand.

She returns to her room, kneels at the bed for her morning lauds. *For the needs of those who are confused. For the needs of those who are without hope. For the needs of those who have no one to pray for them.*

It is still dark when she hears the clatter of cutlery and the whistle of the kettle. He sits bleary-eyed at the breakfast table.

—For you, he says, guiding a file across the Formica table.

She fingers the sharp edge of the folder, then turns to the first page. Ian has printed out all the information he can find from the Internet. Three pictures of Carlos, one a headshot, one with government ministers, one taken outside the Institute for Peace.

—His name is Euclides Largo. I mean, that's what he calls himself.

—Euclides.

—Fifty-nine years old. He's with a small left-wing party.

—That can't be.

—I've been researching all night. They've a lot of support in the countryside, it seems. They're left wing.

—But he's right wing. I mean that's . . .

—Go figure.

—Are they Catholic, his party?

—They don't seem—I don't know, I don't think so. Who knows? I'm sorry, Bev. All I can tell is that he's moved up through the ranks over the years.

A surge of bitterness at the base of her spine.

—He was a lawyer before he got into politics. His main thrust is coal mining. He represents the miners. Copper deposits, corporate access to the mines, that sort of thing. He makes his argument for peace on the basis of economics.

She drags the file a little closer and runs her fingers along the edge of his photograph. She has a sudden urge for a cigarette: she has not craved one in days.

To smoke, to cough, to burn and disappear.

—It's him.

—Are you sure?

She is pierced by the thought that it is all a delusion stacked against her faith, a test of her ability to believe.

—Sure as God, she says.

—You could go to the newspapers.

—And what?

—I can call some friends at the radio station. The embassy. You should call the embassy—

—And say what?

—He raped you, Bev.

—Thirty-seven years ago.

A trapezoid of morning light crosses the kitchen floor. She hears a shout from farther along the street and a blast of laughter, then the smash of a bottle on the pavement: so early, so late.

Ian rises to the kitchen window to part the curtains to look down the length of the street.

—Hooligans, he says.

He waits at the curtains, opening and closing them as if there is some Morse code that he might reveal to the street below.

—You don't still smoke, do you? she asks.

He shuffles into the living room, returns moments later with a small blue bag of tobacco and rolling papers. He fumbles with the paper, licks the edge, smooths it down, passes her the roll-up, takes a box of matches from the kitchen drawer. The smell of sulfur jags her awake.

———

IT IS A FOUR-STORY townhouse fronted by a black ironwork fence, on the eastern side of the river. The walls of the Institute look recently painted, perfectly white. Flowerpots in the windowsills with red flowers, hydrangeas. A large brass plate on the wall. She had expected something grander, more surprising. Nobody gathered outside. No mothers with placards. No cameras or waiting limousines.

A feeble rain drizzles down. She stands at the curb and looks up to see the dark outline of a lamp in the front window. The vague shadows of figures crossing and recrossing the room. It strikes her as a place more of silence than peace. She is at the door before she even catches herself. Her hand on the intercom button. The buzzer sounds. She glances up at the security camera. A silence and then a second buzzing. Longer, more insistent, impatient even.

—Can I help you?

What vanity brought me here, what conceit? She sees a shape in the window, someone looking out at her.

—Sorry, she says into the intercom.

She turns her face into her damp headscarf, descends the steps, walks quickly away, an old woman, the cost weighed in every tendon.

At a corner sandwich shop, she stops. Newspapers on a rack outside. An Irish paper too: she has not seen one in many years. The red light of a camera blinks as she steps inside. She buys the paper and a coffee, sits at the counter to read.

From a distance she watches the front of the Institute, the quiet comings and goings, the shapes of shapes.

The hours drift. The shop is quiet. She scans the paper, even the sports pages, but cannot recall a single word of what she has read.

In the late afternoon she stops at the church in Westminster. From his accent the priest is young, African. Formal. Correct. Mannered. Even in the darkness she can tell he is one who stiffens his collar. She has, she says, failed in the most ordinary way to embrace forgiveness. She has lied about her whereabouts to others. She has failed His grace. She has spent her time in sloth. She has not sought out her fellow Sisters in London, nor any solace from her family within the Church. She has missed her duties: mass, prayer, the holy sacrament. She is unsure now if any of her service is toward the Lord.

It is, in the end, she thinks, the shallowest of confessions: all of the truth, none of the honesty.

After penance, she wanders out into the city, along the Thames. The river sweeps by, turbulent and bulging, but without sound.

In Ian's apartment she moves out from his room, allows him his double bed. She takes a blanket to the couch. She sleeps, surrounded by books.

BEVERLY REPEATS THE RITUAL three days in a row, standing outside the Institute, waiting, watching, shuffling away, her headscarf pulled tight. In the sandwich shop she sits on a swivel stool at the counter, from which she can see through the window the length of the street. Always a flurry of activity in the morning. Black cars. A series of shapes hustling up the steps. The lights inside flickering on and off. At lunchtime, too, the men and women coming down the steps. From a distance any number of them could be him. In the evening, when the dark descends, it is harder to tell, the street shiny with rain, the lamplight carrying the shapes away.

It seems to her that she could sit here for seasons on end: watching the street leaf and unleaf itself.

Decades ago, in Bogotá, there had been a time when she waited for a bus to return her to the village. She remained in the station for two and a half days. Diesel fumes. The screech of brakes. She sat on a wooden bench, clutching her ticket. She had not eaten and carried only a small flask of water. She read from the scriptures. Peter the Apostle. Manacled to that same post. The Mamertine.

On the fifth day she sees him.

It is late afternoon. She sits in the corner of the shop, her hands curled around a cold coffee cup. The newspaper is spread out in front of her. The headlines of a foreign country. The shop is quiet, monitored by the series of cameras set up high around the corners.

She is about to finish her coffee and return to Ian's apartment when the bell sounds out on the door.

A gust of cold wind. The small hint of a cough. She bends

forward and grips the counter. He glides past her. It takes a moment to even realize that it is him. The back of his hair is perfectly combed. His suit is rumpled but smart. There is a click from the heels of his shoes. At the fridge he takes out a cold coffee drink. He has, under his arm, a Spanish-language paper. Why did she not see him walking along the street? Where has he appeared from? He says something, she is sure, to the Pakistani shopkeeper: she cannot quite hear. He drops a coin in the small tray at the side of the register.

She removes her dark cardigan, folds it in her lap, swivels on the chair, places her hands in the well of her skirt, watches him in the shop-window reflection, all of him reversed, right to left.

A smell of aftershave rolls from him as he passes. Is it enough to have seen him? To just be here? I should allow myself, in the obedience of faith, to be used by God's love. Make of myself a prayerful absence.

She reaches out to tug the side of his jacket. The flap end, close to his hip. The cloth feels so terribly expensive.

He turns. A surge of heat pulses through her. A bristling of the hair on her arms. World without end. The mole on his cheek. The tilt of his eye.

—Euclides Largo?

—Yes?

She can tell straight away that he has become the sort of man who is happy to be recognized. His skin has grown lighter, as if he has come indoors, drawn the curtains on that other life. He arches an eyebrow, reaches out a political hand. She does not take it. She grips her cardigan instead. No language at all. To bless him now, to forgive him, to let him go on his way?

—You're at the Institute?

—Yes.

—I saw you on television. Spanish language. In New York.

—A wonderful city.

He favors the door a moment, glances outside, but then turns: And you are . . . ?

—I'm just—an interested observer.

He leans back as if to put her in focus.

—Journalist?

—I'm far too old to be interested in journalism. I'm just watching from a distance, Mr. Largo.

—But you speak Spanish?

—Just a little.

He peels back the cellophane tab from the lid of the drink, taps the bottom of the container against the heel of his hand. It strikes her that he wears no rings on his fingers. No marriage, then, no children.

A tightness cramps her chest when he brings the coffee to his mouth. She lets out a small sound: something trapped, hidden. He nods as if about to leave, but she leans forward on the stool. Am I supposed to directly bestow my forgiveness, Lord? Am I to reconcile with evil? Is that what is being asked of me? Is that what You demand after all these years? *Apokatastasis panton.* The restoral of all things. To what, then, shall I be restored? Is there no wisdom? Is that what I have to learn? That there is finally none at all?

It has, she notices, begun to rain outside, a steady patter against the window.

She speaks slowly, the words emerging, small stones of sound: The television said you're working at the draft of a treaty?

—We are.

—You're aligned with the miners?

—And their families, sí. We're struggling, but we are, how you say, we are getting along, bit and bit. We'll have a statement—

—Poco a poco.

—So, you do speak Spanish?

—It's coming back to me. And your English? It's good now.

—Excuse me?

—Your English is good now, Carlos.

She stands. She is a full head taller than him. Still she does not offer her hand.

—Excuse me?

—It's good, Carlos. Your English.

—Euclides, he says. Largo.

—Sister Beverly Clarke, she says.

He glances over his shoulder toward a waiting car outside, a small fan of smoke rising from its exhaust, the rain bouncing off the roof. Two young boys enter the shop: when they remove their hoods one of them looks remarkably to her like the boy who played the piano in Victoria Station.

—You've become a man of peace, Carlos.

—I'm not sure—excuse me—I think you've maybe mistaken me—

—I don't think so.

—You must excuse me. I have a car waiting.

It strikes her how ordinary and extraordinary both, then, this moment, a street-corner shop, the rain, a London sidestreet, her rapist, thirty-seven years ago, the sound of a distant piano, a pigeon flapping through a railway station, her brother, the books on the floor, a collision, that ancient river in Galway where she made her decision to join the Church, so young then, the way the light shone even on the underside of the bridge, bouncing up from the copper-colored Owenriff.

—I'm not here to hurt you, Carlos. You have more important things to do. I'm not here to ruin what you are doing.

—What is it you said your name was again?

—Sister Beverly Clarke.

—Well, Sister Beverly Clarke, it's a pleasure to meet you, but I think you've mistaken me—

—But I'd like to know how you achieved it.

—I'm afraid you're wasting your time.

—Where did you find it, Carlos? That grace?

—Encantado. Let me go. My jacket. You're holding my jacket.

Beverly is surprised to feel the tug in her fingers, that it is true, she has brought him closer, that there is the faint smell of coffee from his breath, that she has bridged this space, caught him so unaware.

She lets go of him, hears the high ping of the cash register and the fumble for money, a laugh from one of the young boys as they leave the shop.

—Do you recognize me?

—Por supuesto no le . . .

She touches the top button on her blouse, opens it. He steps back, attempts an ease into his face.

—Are you sure, Carlos?

—No me llame Carlos.

—I'm interested in what it means to you. When you sit there and you talk about peace?

A second button, the necklace at her fingers. The shopkeeper has not moved, his dark hands spread wide on the countertop.

—I would be happy to talk to you in my office, Miss—

—Sister Beverly.

—You could arrange it with my secretary.

—You're doing good work, Carlos.

—Stop it.

—I'm not going to harm that.

He leans toward her: No sé quién diablo eres, tu.

She opens the third button on her blouse, her flesh cold to the touch. He turns, panicked, toward the shopkeeper, then glances back to Beverly.

—No puedes hacer esto.

—It healed, see?

—Soltame.

No embarrassment. No shame. She is surprised by the banality of it, how naked, how ordinary it is to her, the small ruin of her breast in her hand.

—Que quieres conmigo?

—Nothing.

—Tell me what you want.

—Nothing, Carlos. Nothing. I just want you to know that I'm here, I exist, that's all.

He backs, panicked, toward the door. A small hitch in his step as he leaves. He grasps for the handle. The door swings slowly closed behind him.

She watches through the window as Carlos yanks open the rear door of a car. Something apparitional in the moment. A man immune to himself. It looks to her as if he is stepping into a caisson of his own loneliness. He slams the door. The tinted window powers down.

She begins to rebutton her blouse.

From the rear seat Carlos stares out. He gestures with an open hand and the car lurches forward, the small rope of exhaust fumes dispersing into the air.

Five yards along the car stops again and the door opens. His suit jacket swings in the wind. He steps over the curb, his hands above his head as if he might stop the rain.

The shop bell sounds again. The top of his shoes are wet and dripping. He stands, his face red, the veins in his neck shining. Something shifting and buzzing in his eyes.

He looks up at the shop ceiling, turns his back to the camera. So, he does not want to be seen, then. For how many years has he walked in this wilderness?

He leans forward, a sheen of sweat or rain on his brow, she can't tell which. He hovers a moment close to her, his breath sharp in her ear.

—Puta, he whispers.

The word is immediately meek and useless. It grazes against her, dissolves, tumbles, something graceful even about its fall.

Beverly turns her back, steps toward the counter, the tea, her newspaper. No nerves in her fingers. No shake in her hands. She closes the final button of her blouse.

She is aware, now, exactly what sort of man he has become. No peace about him. No great swerve in his life. He has polished all his lies.

She could, now, do anything at all: arrange a conference, expose him to the newspapers, call him to task, let others know, create a revenge out of justice. But she will, she knows, just sit at the counter, slowly sip her tea, let the minutes pass, fold the newspaper, rise, leave the shop, shuffle down along the Thames, return to her brother's flat, sit with him, talk, allow the night to fade away, and later she will slip into the warm bath, rise, towel, glance at the mirror, look away again, dress, sleep in the chair instead of the bed, listen to the evening tap against the windowpane, rise then, leave, return to Houston, a long flight across the Atlantic, a return, up the steps, those young girls, that small bakery of love and death.

There is a silence behind her, then she hears the sound of the shop door closing, a car door, an engine, and Carlos is gone.

Beverly runs her finger around the rim of the saucer, folds the newspaper, smooths out the creases, moves toward the cash register. Rows of cigarettes, lottery tickets, sweets. She slides the folded newspaper across the counter. She will leave the paper for the shopkeeper now, allow him to sell it again, why not: she has no more use for it.

She returns to her seat, ties her headscarf, lifts her coat into her arms.

The shopkeeper remains still, his hands spread wide. There is, she notices, a copy of the Qur'an near the register, thumbed, used. On a black-and-white television screen behind him, she sees the front door of the shop, the aisles of food, a small coin of baldness in the back of his head.

He has about him the air of a man prone to bruises and scars. There is a dark mark in the center of his forehead. A prayer bruise. She feels herself shiver. She has stepped into his world, showed herself immodest.

—Excuse me, sir?

—Madam?

—I'm sorry, she says.

—I didn't see anything, Madam. I assure you. I did not see a thing.

She likes him for the quickness of the lie. She glances up at the ceiling camera.

—Those tapes?

—Yes?

—I don't suppose you could give them to me?

—Excuse me?

—I wouldn't like anybody else to see them.

He seems to ponder it a moment, weigh it. He reaches out and pats the newspaper on the counter, nods at her with a sharp cordiality.

—I'm afraid not. They record on the drive. There's no actual tapes. I can't give them to you.

He touches his hand to his chest where a row of pens sit in his shirt pocket.

—But nobody will see them, I promise you.

Beverly pulls the cardigan around her shoulders, hitches her coat, catches a glimpse of herself in the cubed screens, two or three versions, standing in the store, from the front, from behind, caught in the chorus of light and dark.

She steps through the shop, pauses a moment, spies the reflection of the shopkeeper in the window. At the cash register, the blinking red camera light above him is immutable, almost sacred.

—Thank you, she says without turning.

It is, she recognizes, an agreement of faith with a man whose name she does not even know.

She reaches for the door handle, pulls up the collar of her coat against the chill, steps out to the street and into the hard free fall of rain.

AUTHOR'S NOTE

These stories were primarily completed in 2014 on either side of an incident that occurred in New Haven, Connecticut, on June 27, when I was punched from behind and knocked unconscious, then hospitalized, after trying to help a woman who had also been assaulted in the street.

Some of these stories were written before the assault and some of them were written afterward (for example, the punch in "Thirteen Ways" was dreamed up long before the incident, but Beverly's recognition of her attacker in "Treaty" was written later).

Sometimes it seems to me that we are writing our lives in advance, but at other times we can only ever look back. In the end, though, every word we write is autobiographical, perhaps most especially when we attempt to avoid the autobiographical.

For all its imagined moments, literature works in unimaginable ways.

These stories have their own voices, but to learn more about their provenance, including the Victim Impact Statement from that incident in Connecticut, please go to my website, colummccann.com.

THIRTEEN WAYS
of LOOKING

Colum McCann

A
READER'S
GUIDE

Questions and Topics
for Discussion

1.   The title of this collection comes from the poem "Thirteen Ways of Looking at a Blackbird" by Wallace Stevens, which appears in its entirety throughout the first story. What do you think is the significance of the poem, and why did the author adapt its title for this collection?

2.   McCann has said that his favorite passage from the poem is "I do not know which to prefer,/The beauty of inflections/ Or the beauty of innuendos,/The blackbird whistling/Or just after." How might this passage relate to the theme of surveillance throughout the novella?

3.   The world of the first story, "Thirteen Ways of Looking," is one in which security cameras are everywhere but fail to capture the crucial moment of the attack on Mendelssohn. What do you think is the significance of that failure, and what does it say about how we perceive the truth?

4.   The act and art of storytelling appears in many forms throughout this collection—from the unnamed author crafting

his story in "What Time Is It Now, Where You Are?" to Carlos presenting a new "story" of himself as a supposed agent of peace in "Treaty." What are some other examples? What do these instances of storytelling have in common, and how are they different?

5.   What do you think Beverly is seeking in her trip to London in "Treaty"? Does she find it? Do you agree with her decision not to expose Carlos for who he is? Does she achieve justice or revenge?

6.   Discuss the theme of empathy as it's explored in this collection. What does empathy mean to you? What does it mean to the characters in these stories?

7.   In his author's note, Colum McCann writes, "In the end, . . . every word we write is autobiographical, perhaps most especially when we attempt to avoid the autobiographical." Do you agree or disagree with that statement? How does it affect your reading of the collection?

8.   None of the stories are told in first person, but each has its own distinct voice that brings to life the characters' perspectives. How does the author achieve this? Did you identify with any of the characters more than with others? Why?

9.   Compare and contrast the different ways the author depicts the relationship between a parent and a child throughout

the collection. What does the idea that it's "Impossible to be a child forever. A mother, always" mean to you?

10. The mother in "Sh'khol" struggles to find a translation for the title word, meaning a parent who has lost a child, and eventually realizes that the word is "shadowed." Why do you think that's the word she decides on? Do you agree or disagree?

11. There is a large amount of random violence, loss, and difficulty in these stories. Ultimately, do you think this is an optimistic collection? McCann has said that to be a good optimist one must be "muscular enough to refuse cynicism." What do you think he means by this?

12. Each of the four stories is written in thirteen sections. There is a very conscious structure at play, but it's subtle, particularly in "Sh'khol" and "Treaty." Why do you think that is? Do you think being aware of that structure as a reader would take away from the spontaneity of the stories?

13. What would your own thirteenth question be?

COLUM MCCANN is the internationally bestselling author of the novels *TransAtlantic, Let the Great World Spin, Zoli, Dancer, This Side of Brightness,* and *Songdogs;* as well as the critically acclaimed story collections *Thirteen Ways of Looking, Everything in This Country Must,* and *Fishing the Sloe-Black River.* His fiction has been published in thirty-five languages. He has received many honors, including the National Book Award, the International IMPAC Dublin Literary Award, a Chevalier des Arts et des Lettres award from the French government, and the Ireland Fund of Monaco Literary Award in Memory of Princess Grace. He has been named one of *Esquire*'s "Best and Brightest," and his short film *Everything in This Country Must* was nominated for an Oscar in 2005. A contributor to *The New Yorker, The New York Times Magazine, The Atlantic,* and *The Paris Review,* he teaches in the Hunter College MFA Creative Writing program. He lives in New York City with his wife and their three children, and he is the cofounder of the global nonprofit story exchange organization Narrative 4.

colummccann.com
Facebook.com/colummcannauthor

To inquire about booking Colum McCann for a speaking engagement, please contact the Penguin Random House Speakers Bureau at speakers@penguinrandomhouse.com.

This book was set in Fournier, a typeface named for Pierre-Simon Fournier (1712–68), the youngest son of a French printing family. He started out engraving woodblocks and large capitals, then moved on to fonts of type. In 1736 he began his own foundry and made several important contributions in the field of type design; he is said to have cut 147 alphabets of his own creation. Fournier is probably best remembered as the designer of St. Augustine Ordinaire, a face that served as the model for the Monotype Corporation's Fournier, which was released in 1925.

Chat.
Comment.
Connect.

Visit our online book club community at
Facebook.com/RHReadersCircle

Chat
Meet fellow book lovers and discuss what you're reading.

Comment
Post reviews of books, ask—and answer—thought-provoking
questions, or give and receive book club ideas.

Connect
Find an author on tour, visit our author blog, or invite one of
our 150 available authors to chat with your group on the phone.

Explore
Also visit our site for discussion questions, excerpts, author
interviews, videos, free books, news on the latest releases,
and more.

Books are better with buddies.
Facebook.com/RHReadersCircle